Svetlana Konantseva

The poison of sin

Ironic phytodetective

How often the inexplicable and mysterious haunt us in everyday life? Sometimes we simply do not have the strength, time and desire to look closely at the surrounding reality and ask ourselves this question.

The main heroine of the story, Jeanne, was drawn into the investigation of a series of deaths in the family of her close friend Masha. For several years, fate brought her friends together until they came closer to solving a terrible secret ...

«All things are poison, and
there is nothing without poison,
only the dose makes the thing non-toxic».
Paracelsus

Chapter 1. Acquaintance

June 2020, Vologda

What drives us and makes us commit rash acts? Was it necessary to go to Aunt Galya in June ?! But on the other hand, summer is passing. It is not often that nature pampers us, the inhabitants of the Russian North, with good weather and warmth. Therefore, I really do not want to lose the precious days of my favorite season.

In Petersburg, the masquerade caused by the pandemic has subsided. To tell the truth, not really anyone bothered with the imposed restrictions. In Vologda, I found myself in a different reality.

For about forty minutes I stuck on the platform in line for the tent, proudly called a checkpoint. There, people of dubious neatness tried to take swabs for the "new coronavirus infection", found out addresses, passwords and turnouts, phone numbers. Everywhere they are already limited to remote measurement of body temperature, but not in Vologda. And with such a total demonstrative control, the deputy vigilant governor and his wife manage to get sick with COVID-19 and worsen the statistics of the region. True, the deputy in his interview palely justifies that he contracted the virus when he was with his wife on vacation in Italy.

I am sincerely sorry for ordinary Vologda residents, who have been extended the mask regime until August, while the top officials of the region enjoy their rest, travel the world and do not deny themselves anything.

I did not think that I would live to see the time when the phrase "He does not have everything at home" would sound like a denunciation.

However, all this is lyrics. I went to the second week of self-isolation, they even called me once with a check, and I confirmed directly by phone that I had isolated myself from the outside world in every possible way.

There is already a joke on the Internet about self-isolation. "At first, the slogan was self-employment. Then - self-education. Now - self-isolation. Self-medication tomorrow. Then - self-destruction ... ". I would like to avoid the latter.

Of course, I had to go to the store, but as a law-abiding citizen, I, like many other customers, shyly covered the most vulnerable place for the virus, my chin.

So today, I go to the store, bothering no one, and towards me a man of indeterminate age, smoothly striving for sixty. He is approaching me purposefully, eyes glowing with blue flame, gray curls fluttering in the wind. Of course, I am a beauty, but I can hardly arouse such fanatical interest in my person.

- In two hours the sky will fall to the ground! - He exclaimed and looked intently into my eyes.

It seems crazy, it's better not to argue with them. He is excited and clearly expects something from me. I raise my gaze to the sky and so calmly speak:

- Not. Will not fall, will not fall ... Not today, - the voice trembled treacherously. Didn't seem to notice, the eyes went out, the excitement subsided, the man walked past, going about his business. Carried.

I went to the store. I stood there, examining the goods, thinking what to do with something like that. Nearby is a granny at a shelf with cereals, talking to someone. A decent-looking old woman, neatly dressed, combed, reticule in her hands. I looked closely at her. An elderly lady conducted a dialogue with a bag of semolina.

- What have you become so dear? Yesterday it cost twenty-eight rubles more, and today it was seven-ten-two. And tomorrow what to expect from you?

And, indeed, semolina for seventy-two rubles for eight hundred grams!

- You go to a nearby store, it seems, there is semolina for thirty-two rubles, - I turned with advice to the old woman.

- I won't take you, I'll go to the next store, there the groats are not so impudent, - and it was she who continued the conversation with the semolina.

I walked to the checkout, past apples, and there were apples at one hundred and eighty rubles per kilogram, yesterday they were seventy-nine. I caught myself thinking that I wanted to ask them a question. No, it's all! Paying and home.

I return back to the courtyards. Around the panel five-story buildings from the times of the Brezhnev stagnation. Once upon a time, these were green, cozy courtyards with benches, children's swings and sandpits. In recent years, small distances between houses are gradually rolling into asphalt, turning into parking lots for local residents.

I saw that there was a small tent behind the container platform. So what is trading? In it, two aunts huddle in bags of covering material, wearing masks and blue gloves. In front of them is a transparent plastic box on a table the size of a stool. A little to the side, a bearded boy and a girl are trampling on. No, you don't think anything like that, girl without a beard. Young people are also wearing masks and gloves, while outside +25 degrees Celsius, obviously, they are not just soaring.

I remembered! The same vote goes on amendments to the Constitution of the Russian Federation. Television advertising on all channels. Famous and not so famous people are trying to convince us of the need to change the text of the Constitution.

Incidentally, I read these amendments, complete nonsense. And before the Basic Law of the country was not particularly observed, it is, perhaps, of a declarative nature. And now nothing will change. It is necessary to write this: "The Russian Federation, united by a thousand-year history, preserving the memory of ancestors who passed on to us ideals and faith in God ...". What God, comrades? Although no, now not comrades, but citizens and civilians! The Russian Federation is a secular state, multinational. Secular does not mean attending social events, as many schoolchildren think and, it seems, not only them. In a secular state, you can profess any religion or not profess any.

However, politics is not mine.

I look at this farce, and stupid rhymes come into my head. I'll write it down now.

***

Vote all week
By the trash heap, on the bench,
Put ballots in the ballot boxes,
Vote at polling stations.
The choice "For" - it is extremely difficult,
There will be the same "crap" and Putin.

When I read this speech to my friend - the famous Yamal designer - Galina Koyalkhot, she appreciated my work:

- If it is the 37th year, you will be sent to harvest reeds.

Well, if such a thing, in relation to the current situation in the country, the ditty, which has become a popular one, is perfect: "Vote - don't vote, you will get x anyway." The result is the same.

While running to the store, quarantine in the Vologda region was once again extended until July 13. It seems that this madhouse will never end. No wonder the name of the local governor is consonant with the name of the psychiatric hospital in Vologda.

My aunt is a lonely woman; we love to chat in the evenings over a cup of tea. But, being an "owl", she sleeps until one o'clock, so the morning is at my complete disposal.

By the way, I make tea myself, guided by my mood and state of health.

Upon arrival in Vologda, I already ran to a nearby suburb. I know one place where there are gorgeous rose hips beyond the field. They say that during the time of Ivan the Terrible, the price of a rosehip was equal to the value of precious stones and metals, as well as satin and velvet. Then the fruits of this plant were considered one of the most valuable medicines, and their collection was constantly monitored, and they were stored in the royal warehouses. June is the time to collect wild rose petals. In addition to the aroma, according to the beliefs of the Greeks, arousing passion, tea made from the petals of this plant has a lot of useful properties.

It strengthens the immune system, helps against colds, strengthens with indigestion and intestinal infections, cleanses the liver, has a beneficial effect on the teeth and gums, helps to normalize the heart rate, cures diseases of the cardiovascular system and has many other useful qualities. Unlike fruits, rosehip petals have practically no contraindications. They are used for making infusions, decoctions, teas, syrups, jams, liqueurs, oils. But I add dried petals to tea and make a tincture that I use for cosmetic purposes. To prepare the tincture ("rose water"), I dip fresh rosehip petals into a bottle and fill it with vodka, then insist in a dark place for three weeks and filter. A wonderful, fragrant lotion is ready!

Today I drank tea with wild rose petals, a leaf of lemon balm and a pinch of purchased black Ceylon large leaf, and I remembered that I forgot to introduce myself.

My name is Zhanna Romanovna Veresova. For the last fifteen years I have been living in St. Petersburg, I have no permanent job, I write phytotherapeutic articles for dubious Internet publishers. I am young, at least at heart, quite attractive, in my opinion, a woman. Slender, intelligent, at this stage, brown-haired.

By diploma I am a teacher of chemistry and biology. On this occasion, I remembered an anecdote:

The wife laments:

- You bastard! Ruined my whole life! I spent all my youth on you...

The husband soothes:

- Honey, stops talking with a diploma.

Maybe my diploma is not the most unfortunate acquisition in my life, but I spent five years on it, and it never met my expectations.

I worked in my specialty for only a year.

I remember this year as a rather unpleasant dream.

Pupils who do not need anything, some of whom simply due to limited mental abilities cannot study in a general education school, while others realized the uselessness and unnecessary information of most of the school curriculum.

Tired teachers who are tired of lack of money, of the meaninglessness of paperwork, which takes the time necessary for quality preparation for lessons.

Now the teacher does not bear the light and eternal, does not enlighten the people, but provides educational services.

Therefore, they treat teachers as service personnel. Neither pupils, nor their parents, nor the school administration, nor the state itself respect them.

To get the minimum wage promised by the President, teachers take two rates and either sew up and die at work, or do not care about it.

It is especially unpleasant to remember the school administration, which is insolent from its small power and impunity.

There I saw the women's team in all its glory.

Beaten by life, disgruntled aunts in baggy practical rags, not daring to have an opinion. To be fair, I want to note that there were a couple of professionals among them, they just were not lucky enough to be in this school, like me. Small intrigues due to a hundred rubles of a bonus, a willingness to play dirty tricks, make noise, curry favor.

"Divide and conquer on the scale of a chicken coop!" - The motto of the head teacher and director.

These intriguing professionals had a lot to learn. For example, the head teacher for educational work, an important stout aunt, walked around with a smart look and taught how to teach lessons. She herself demonstrated aerobatics, taught Russian language lessons simultaneously in two classes, a kind of prototype of distance learning. It is not surprising that among the students of this "professional" I have not met those who are able to competently express their thoughts.

The head teacher for academic work and the schedule is just boorish cattle, moreover, an extremely vindictive person.

The headmistress brilliantly threw dust in her eyes, seemingly a decent intelligent woman, and in fact gave a head start to her deputies.

For many years they drove the school to the bottom of the ranking of educational institutions, the turnover was terrible every year five to seven subject students changed, that is, teachers of various disciplines. It's a pity that they were dispersed only the next academic year after I left..

But these people demonstrated to me by their example the basic law of the universe: you have to pay for everything in this life. Take the headmistress. She abused the power not only for the sake of self-interest, she dishonored meanly, on the sly. I pitted people, did not think about the psychological climate of the school, permeated with hostility. When people ran out of school, I tried to catch up on bad reviews and characteristics. And she herself, in fact, is an unhappy woman. She gave birth to a child late, after a fleeting holiday romance. A disabled child whom she hid and was ashamed of. She did not enjoy the authority of her colleagues. Friendly, let alone romantic, did not evoke feelings. When the staff turnover exceeded all reasonable limits, she was transferred to an ordinary teacher, and there she was lost.

Oddly enough, it was in this godforsaken school that I met Masha. She also came to get a job that year and plunged into the world of "anti-school". Maria Vladimirovna looked like a fragile, shy teenager. The shortsighted look gave her a touch of unfaithfulness in herself. She has an intelligent face, a high forehead, large expressive eyes, a clear Roman-Greek profile, light fluffy hair of a dark chocolate shade. Masha practically did not use cosmetics, except perhaps with mascara and lip gloss. But under this angelic guise was a strong-willed man, sometimes uncompromising, able to insist on his own, possessing the gift of an orator, the ability to convince, explain, transform, bewitch. She gave the impression of a calm, balanced person, but this is due to the efforts of will and endurance. A volcano of passion inside. Sometimes it could be carried over.

In order not to drown in the negative microclimate of the educational institution, we united and made friends. Ur partisan war to preserve our personality and ideals of pedagogy united us for many years. It was from Masha that I learned the methodology of teaching the subject, despite the fact that she led economics and social studies. Play activities, the work of students in pairs and groups, reading poetry, trying to make children think and reason, all this looked somewhat wild in a pedagogically neglected school.

If not for her, I would have escaped in a month.

We held out for the academic year, but did not join the team and left.

In the summer my aunt's friend offered me a job as a specialist in the archive.

What does the presence of a chemical and biological education have to do with working in an archive, you ask? Yes, the most direct! Marusya with her East Faculty diploma (she graduated from the university with a degree in History) would never have been taken there. Who needs a specialist with a specialized education and an excellent "cooking pot" who can compete with the leaders? Moreover, Masha had no connections, while my aunt Gali did. So I started working in the archive. This is Vologda, in every state office the same thing, "ours and ours."

In a quiet, peaceful atmosphere of dusty shelves, I met my Volodya. In 2003, it was not yet as fashionable as it is now, to study the history of a kind. Today everyone is striving to prove their noble origins; they see themselves as descendants of kings, nobles or merchants, at worst.

Last year, when I went to my previous place of work to visit a good friend, I witnessed a rather curious, but very revealing case.

A man with a delay, if not mental, and then speech development, turned to the archive room, for sure. His appearance was remarkable. Narrow forehead, protruding brow ridges, flattened skull, depressed nose, snaggy figure with disproportionately long arms. True, he was dressed decently, richly.

In a fashionable suit with a tie and expensive boots, the man looked very impressive. Only after a few minutes of his incoherent speech did it become clear that he wanted to study his ancestry. To this he was politely replied that they could enroll him in the reading room, the waiting line would be 90 days. The man made it clear that he did not know how to work with archival materials at all. Personally, I generally doubted his ability to read. Considering his appearance and speech, my imagination vividly drew to itself his ancestors, dexterously climbing trees in search of bananas, or the ancient Hyperboreans who had escaped from the zoo, inhabiting the vastness of the Russian North.

Forty thousand rubles, for which the young fair-haired employee of the archive promised to compile his family tree with noble roots, seemed to me an insignificant amount. The client was ready to pay for the service immediately:

- You card ...? Cash ...? Can I use rubles?

- What are you, only after completing the order, - modestly lowering her eyes, the employee whispered loudly, fearfully looking around. "Call in three months," she held out a vid.

- What's so long? - The visitor was genuinely perplexed.

- We have a lot of orders, - the girl answered politely.

The reading room was indeed filled with visitors, many of whom I had met before. Only then did they collect materials for their scientific works, and now they carried out orders for drawing up genealogies.

- So, come on, I will pay extra for the urgency, - suggested the client.

- What are you, it is not supposed to be, - and the employee was embarrassed.

- Well, okay, - the visitor sighed and went home.

And in 2003, people were just studying their ancestry, not for the sake of fame and not for the sake of money, purely out of scientific curiosity. It is on the basis of interest in the historical fate of our ancestors that we became close to Volodya. In 2004 I left the archive, left Vologda and moved to my husband in St. Petersburg. But that's a completely different story ...

Chapter 2. Meeting at the hospital

September 2014, Vologda

In early September, I was going to visit my aunt Galya.

It so happened that at the age of seventeen I lost my parents, and my mother's sisters - Galina and Nadezhda - as they could, replaced them for me.

August was an extremely difficult month for me morally, my husband and I decided to undergo IVF. Feeling the need to change the situation, I rushed to Vologda. Working as a laboratory assistant at a research institute where my husband taught did not really bother me. Basically, I might not work at all. But formal employment has three main advantages: Friday, salary and vacation.

Aunt Nadia lamented apples and vegetables for us. All day I cut and dried apples in the dryer, and Galina did home preservation. In the evenings on Skype we talked with Volodya. Everything was calm and quiet.

On Thursday morning, I felt pain in the lower abdomen, called an ambulance. I was taken to the regional gynecology. And imagine my surprise, there I saw Masha. She was admitted in a state of hemorrhagic shock caused by severe blood loss. In the corridor, a friend lost consciousness, she was transported to the ward, put on a drip, like with artificial blood, with something transparent, brought her to her senses, literally an hour later operated on, removed the myoma node, the birth of which caused profuse bleeding. Until the evening she laid under an IV, all day she was injected with something, then plasma, then erythrocyte suspension.

In the morning Marusya walked briskly to breakfast, and after going around her they transferred her to my room. I was prescribed injections and pills, and my friend was prescribed only iron preparations.

We haven't seen each other for so many years, but here is such a meeting and such a place ?! But the ways of the Lord are inscrutable, as they say.

- How did you, Mashunya, come to such a life?

- Belief in Russian medicine let me down, Janet. Before the operation, the doctors made fun of me that people like me only come from the tundra and from the antenatal clinic on Arkhangelskaya Street. I applied for medical help back in the summer of 2013, barely went to these appointments, hemoglobin dropped to 45 units... The gynecologist from the consultation looked competent, she will take the analysis, I am waiting for the result. And she then goes on vacation, then to refresher courses, then postpones the record, then she has holidays.- Treatment, as I understand it, did not offer any?

- Naturally! - Masha snorted.

- Just like in a joke.

The patient asks: "Doctor, how can I cure this?"

The doctor replies: "I'll google it now."

"Or maybe I myself?"

"Come on, patient, let's not self-medicate!"

- And I got something similar, - agreed a friend. - Also with queues. I also remembered anecdote.

The father asks his son: "How was your day?"

"Today they played doctor in kindergarten," the son replied.

"And How?" - The father was interested.

The son replied: "I sat in the corridor under the door for half a day."

"Nothing changes in our medicine," I stated.

- Only one local therapist, - continued Masha, - treated me with understanding. He looks so closely and says: "Hemoglobin 45, you are pale, can hardly walk, shortness of breath, but the brain is still working. Very interesting".

- What about you? - I asked.

- Well, they didn't even take me for a planned operation in such a state, so I began to be treated as best I could.

I drank a decoction of young needles with chaga (then burdock root, then calendula), ate a pinch of cranberries three times a day at the same time as the

Maltofer tablet. She followed an anti-anemic diet: meat, beef liver, buckwheat, red wine, pomegranates. I did medical gymnastics according to Norbekov. On critical days, she saved herself with a tincture of water pepper and a decoction of nettle. Hemoglobin increased to 100 units. A week ago, Aunt Sveta, the one from Gryazovets, my mother's sister, brought me an antitumor tincture; they drink from one to forty drops. I drank it for seven days, reached seven drops, and bleeding opened, called an ambulance, then ... you know", my friend sighed heavily.

- It seems that I did everything right, but I still would not drink the tincture, not prepared with my own hands. You can't imagine how frightened I was when I saw you unconscious on a chair in the hall! - I complained.

- They brought me to the hospital still vigorously, but while they were formalizing, examining, my strength began to leave my mortal body. I myself went to the second floor by elevator, accompanied by a nurse, while they were being identified in the ward, sat down. The weakness is terrible; the heart beats so that it gives off in the ears. And as I sat down on a chair, such lightness surged, it became so calm ... I feel pulled into a tunnel of some kind. And now the light, bright, dazzling, very close, just a little bit more, and everything is behind ... But then a sense of duty woke up in me: "But what about the children, what will become of them?" Then a voice in my head summed up: "It's not time yet." After that I regained consciousness, in the ward I am lying under an IV, - Masha switched to a whisper.

- And you know, in order to prevent the recurrence of the tumor, drink the fly agaric tincture. At the same time, you will strengthen your immunity. In general, a useful thing in the household! The joint ached or the back pulls, rubbed with tincture and forgot. Pigmented spots appeared, wen, moisten cotton wool and apply.

- Isn't it poisonous? - Marusya was surprised.

- You're not just going to eat it? In order to poison them, you need to eat three kilograms. Although with your weight of 47 kg, maybe two is enough? - I began to doubt.

- I just remembered a joke about mushroom poisoning, - the girlfriend smiled.

- The toxicologist asks his friend: "Borya, what's going on with you? Your mother-in-law has been poisoned by mushrooms for the third time this month! "

His friend replies: "Oh, this is all her damned sclerosis: she cooks for me, and then forgets and tries it herself!"

"Even in jokes, they don't die of mushroom poisoning," I said through laughter and, laughing, continued.

- According to all available scientific sources today, not a single lethal outcome has been described over the past 100 years after eating red fly agarics, - here I remembered one story that my grandmother told and shared with Masha.

- My grandmother had a neighbor in the village, her husband bothered her very much, drank, worked from under a cane, and by the age of sixty he also fell ill, when he was not drunk as a lord, everything was whining with pain. Tired of it specifically! She collected fly agarics, and fried him for lunch, and put the bottle at last. He persuaded the whole frying pan for vodka, and she went to a neighboring village to visit with an overnight stay. He comes the next day, and the man is cheerful and full of energy, everything has ceased to hurt, and I don't want to drink, a new life has begun.

- I also remembered one story, my husband told. One of his acquaintances went into the forest for mushrooms, collected two packages, one with redheads (red aspen), the second with fly agarics. I cleaned everything at home and laid it out on baking trays, and went to work myself. On that day, his mother came to visit, as always without warning, appeared. I cleaned up the bachelor's apartment and decided to pamper my son with mushrooms and potatoes. She didn't know much about mushrooms, so she fried fly agarics. The son returned home, everything was clean and the smell was divine, he realized that Mom was visiting. Without second thoughts, he sat down at the table, tasted potatoes with mushrooms and lay down to sleep. In his dreams, he got into the prehistoric world, experienced the brightest impressions in his entire life. Different dragons lived in this world; he understood their thoughts, communicated with them telepathically and even flew on one of them. Everything was so real: a riot of colors, smells, feelings, sensations! He realized that his place is there, and there is a real life filled with meaning, there is his purpose! He no longer experimented with mushrooms, but longing for another world did not leave him ...

- It's like in a joke about a strange forest in which you first go for mushrooms, and then they follow you. And what happened to your husband's acquaintance? - Curiosity arose in me.

- He died in a couple of years, - Masha answered.

- I hope he got where he wanted? ...

I read that the fly agaric is a means that facilitates the vision of another world, allowing you to get there illegally. Illegal invasion of otherworldly worlds entails retribution. Not only physical, intoxication of the body and its consequences, but also spiritual, no one knows where you will be "taken", and what will happen to your consciousness afterwards...

In folklore, the fly agaric is the food of witches, for example, Baba Yaga. Shamans consider him the king of all mushrooms. By the way, according to folk Russian omens, if there are numerous fly agarics in the forest, then there are also enough other mushrooms. The king of mushrooms is allowed to be used only by those who, due to their innate abilities, are different from the rest. These people (shamans, witches and others) have a spontaneous ability to ecstasy, which is maintained and developed, but not just out of a whim, but for the sake of the mission that they fulfill. In general, the cult of plants is a secret into which only a select few are privy. Rumor has it that it was from the fly agarics that the divine drink was prepared - Soma. The preparation of the ritual drink of the Aryans was a complex rite: the Red Mushroom, plucked on a full moon, was soaked in water, then squeezed with pressure stones, cleaned through a strainer - a sieve of white virgin sheep wool, diluted with water from sacred springs, mixed with milk and honey, then poured into vessels, accompanying these actions with the reading of hymns of praise, which were given special importance. At the last sounds of sacred spells, a deity entered the foaming drink, and it turned into Soma.

- And I heard that the mysterious drink of the gods was not an infusion of ephedra or fly agarics, not milk vodka, but beer, the secrets of the preparation of which are still kept secret in the remote corners of the Russian North, - my friend objected, -They say that beer was boiled with milk and honey and got intoxicated drink with amazing properties. Svetlana Vasilievna Zharnikova, Candidate of Historical Sciences, wrote about this, with whom I happened to be personally acquainted.

- Maybe so, who knows? What if a secret ingredient was added to this beer - fly agaric? - I suggested.

- Yes, I've heard a lot about its amazing properties! How to prepare fly agaric tincture? - Masha asked.

- Take five medium strong red fly agarics, or rather their hats. Break into pieces in a 0.7 liter bottle, preferably from dark glass. Pour in vodka; keep in a dark place at normal temperature for 21 days, shaking occasionally. Then strain through cheesecloth, again better in a dark glass bottle. Take at night according to the scheme from one to twenty-five drops, and then in the reverse order (from twenty-five to one). To make it not so disgusting, you can seize with a teaspoon of honey or grated carrots. It is better to drink in courses, with a minimum break of a month.

A friend wrote down the tincture recipe.

Then her mother called her, it turns out today, Maria's grandmother died. A friend said that before her death, Anya's grandmother was sick for a long time, she did not get out of bed. When Maroussia was with her for the last time, she complained that she was being bullied. But Aunt Sveta (mother's sister), who lived there in Gryazovets and looked after the old woman, claimed that this was senile insanity and whims. In addition, Masha, grandmother called Valya, which raised doubts about her adequacy.

Maria did not break away from the hospital, the fact came true, and there was someone to see off the grandma on her last journey. She left two daughters and a husband; there was no need for all the grandchildren to be present. Ten days in the hospital flew by unnoticed, especially in good company. We are lucky with the attending physician! Very competent, real professional, Podolskaya Tatiana Anatolyevna. I still remember with gratitude!

Chapter 3. The request of the deceased

March 2015, St. Petersburg – Vologda

At nine in the morning Masha called, woke up, explained something confused, and asked to come.

In the last half of the year, we have been in contact with her regularly. I appreciate her support. If not for her, I'm not sure I would have coped with the grief that befell me at the end of September 2014.

Then I returned from Vologda rested and replenished. A ridiculous car accident claimed the lives of my husband and mother-in-law. The mother-in-law died instantly, and the doctors fought for the life of her husband for three days, but in vain. They took me away from the funeral in an ambulance. I lost my child ...

Just the other day, I entered into inheritance rights. I moved to my mother-in-law's one-room apartment on Vasilyevsky Island, I rented my husband's apartment on Novatorov Boulevard; it turned out to be beyond my strength to live there.

However, I will not talk about it. I'm going to Vologda.

After kissing my aunt Galya, I called Masha.

- Mashunya, hello, I'm here! Come, Aunt Galya is going to Nadezhda in Gryazovets, no one will interfere with our conversation.

- Zhannochka, I'm very glad to hear from you! I'm already flying! - responded a friend.

In the meantime, I bungled dinner, took out a bottle of red wine. Masha came running pale and disheveled.

- I asked you to spend the night; my houses can cope without me.

We exchanged current news, drank a glass of wine.

- What, friend of my harsh days, happened to you? Inject, my curiosity said.

- My aunt died, Svetlana Petrovna, my mother's sister, my godmother, - Marusya answered in a sad tone.

- Wait, she, it seems, was not old yet. What happened? - I was surprised.

- Fifty-eight years should have been celebrated in the summer. They say a stroke, - Masha shrugged.

- It happens, I sympathize, of course. But what worries you so much?

Maria looked at me strangely.

- You don't think anything like that ... She came to me, - continued her friend in a trembling voice.

- When? - I was amazed.

- It was in a dream. The first time that night when my aunt died in the hospital. She asked not to be saddened by her departure. She ran bright videos about her life, the next. I got the impression that the pictures were either southern France or Italy. And she is so young, happy ... she works in some cafe. Aunt in her youth, as long as I remember her, was, so to speak, not of the Soviet model. She dressed fashionably, put on makeup, and always looked after herself. She was above average height, wore shoes with heels and mini. Large mouth, small nose, large eyes, drawn by arrows. Do you remember in Soviet times there were decals with German girls? She reminded me of them. The next time my aunt came to me on the third day after her death. She asked: "Why did they do this to me? Deal with them ".

- With whom? - I did not understand.
- Who specifically did not say. And on the ninth day, the worst dream was that she was trying to get out of the earth. She asks to help her.
- Horror! I exclaimed.
- That's what I mean, - agreed Masha.
- If we put mysticism aside, although anything can happen, try to formulate what was unusual in her death? By the way, did you do an autopsy?
- No, they did not, - answered the girlfriend, then explained, - On this the son and mother of his wife insisted.
"Quite odd considering her age. Remember how it all happened?

It was early March, I was going to visit her. We agreed to meet and called each other on the eve. In the morning I went to the Gryazovets bus, as we drove away from Vologda, I called my aunt. There were long beeps, no one answered the phone. Then the connection was lost. Approaching Gryazovets, I also tried to call. All in vain! Arrived, no one meets. I walked around the city. Finally, I got through. A woman answered me, introduced herself as any - a friend of Svetlana Petrovna. She said that she was visiting her last night, they drank tea. Then Sveta complained that her eyes were getting dark. She felt sick and called an ambulance. The paramedic looked, said nothing wrong, probably poisoning, drink activated charcoal. Aunt lay down, after a few minutes she lost consciousness. An ambulance was called again, she was taken to the hospital, she was diagnosed with a stroke, and she no longer regained consciousness. This Lyuba claimed that that evening she called her son Andrey, he promised to drive up when there was time. I was very surprised that I was not in the know. She knew about my upcoming visit and told my cousin about it. Then I called my brother, he said that he knew about his mother's condition, he would arrive by lunchtime, he didn't need my help, it's better for me to go back to Vologda and not tell anyone about what happened.

- Quite strange, - I doubted.

- For a normal person, yes. But Andryusik is still a fruit! I went to my grandfather Pete, the father of my mother and aunt Sveta. He began to pry why I came alone, without her. I replied that Svetlana had been in the hospital since yesterday evening, I learned about this this morning. His granddaughter ordered not to say anything to anyone, not to meddle in their affairs. My grandfather reacted to this rather calmly, we drank tea, chatted, and he took me to the bus. The next day my aunt passed away, my brother deigned to inform me so that I would inform my mother and sister. I warned my mother the day before, so she had already left for Vologda, ran to our house for a minute, and I took her to the bus to Gryazovets to her father.

- What happened next?

- The funeral. In the morning I arrived early, they were preparing a memorial table. The body was brought to the church for the funeral service directly from the morgue, in a truck with the inscription "Furniture" on board. In the church I met my brother and his wife Lyubochka. Throughout the ceremony she prayed earnestly, holding a candle in each hand, - Masha told and depicted Lyuba's gestures.

- I heard about something like that, two candles at the funeral service, - vague images swarmed in my head, - an attempt to put up protection from the spirit of the deceased.

- Perhaps, "the friend shrugged", then we drove to the cemetery, lowered the coffin into the grave, threw a handful of earth each. The son and wife did not even come to the grave of their mother, they stood on the sidelines.

- So they didn't touch the cemetery soil? Suspicious, - I commented.

- The commemoration was in the apartment of the grandfather, not in the home of the deceased. Instead of an icon, in the red corner there was a portrait of Andryusik's son with Lyubochka. There was not a single snapshot of the deceased.

- What wildness! - I could not restrain myself.

- They sat down, remembered, after that the aunt's son came up with his faithful. The stars honored us with their presence! The grandfather began to gallop around them. Lyubochka's fur coat made of natural fur of an innocently murdered mink cannot be hung in the hallway, its place on the bed in the back room; - Masha was inflamed in her indignation.

- I remembered a joke about a fur coat, - I giggled.

- The son says to his mother: "Mom, do you know how the poor animal suffered so that you would wear this fur coat?"

Mother replies: "Son, you can't talk about dad like that".

- It's funny, - the friend smiled and continued. - Grandfather made them sit in a place of honor. At the table, my brother mumbled something, Lyubochka started a prayer. She seems to have a large repertoire for all occasions. Here's what else bothered me, Love for food did not touch, put a little for decency, drank from my bottle of water, which I took out of my purse. The secular conversations did not work out after their arrival. We didn't bake pancakes; we bought ready-made ones in a local cafe. We recalled Svetlana Petrovna's culinary talents. Her pancakes were always great! Here Lyubochka interjected: "I also bake pancakes very well." They praised the salad that my sister Alena and I made up. She put in again: "I would have done better." To which she had to answer that she did not have the honor to appreciate her culinary talents, since she had never been invited to her house. Even here, at the commemoration of her beloved mother-in-law, she did not present a single culinary masterpiece. Lyubka replied that she and Andrey are "halves of one whole", and since he does not want to invite us into his house, then she is not happy to see us either. You might think that I only dreamed about it!

While Mashunya was indignant, I remembered the famous statement attributed to Faina Georgievna Ranevskaya: "The other half is in the brain, ass and pills. And I was initially whole! " I wonder what, of the above, is her brother's wife? I shared my concerns with Masha, and we agreed on the second point.

- Sister, - continued the story of a friend, - was a little more harsh: "We've been working hard here since the morning, got up at five in the morning to drive up to six, and not at twelve, like some. So have a conscience, if not to thank, then at least not to find fault with what others have done! We are not gathered here for you and Andrey to sing praises and not to please you. We remember a worthy person and want to talk exclusively about him».

- What are they?

- As I later realized, they only needed a reason to leave, and they got it. With an air of offended innocence, they left the memorial table. Then they whispered something to my grandfather for a long time, and left without saying goodbye to the others - Marusya's cheeks were burning with indignation.

- This Lyuba reminds me of someone. How she looks like?

- She was lean, "the friend began to describe," a little over sixty meters, her hair is rough, straight, mouse-colored, her lips are pursed, her bite is horse bite, her nose is sharp with a hump, her eyes are watery when they roll out. Iwashi herring without a can, - she came up with the nickname Mashunya.

- And the surname, by any chance, is not Seledin? - I seem to have guessed who we are talking about.

- Yes, this is her maiden name; - Masha was surprised at my awareness.

- She studied at the Vologda Pedagogical University at the Faculty of Natural Geography? - My doubts have disappeared.

- Exactly, works as a chemistry teacher in the seventh school.

- I know this little thing; I posed as a princess of blue bloods - BNS (Bore, nerd, snitch). My classmates and I quickly brought this "star" to clean water! A girl from Kubensky told us about her aristocratic roots.

Mother Lyubina graduated from the cultural enlightenment-chilische, worked in the Kubensky Palace of Culture. She gave birth to a girl; it is not known from whom, we are talking about Lyubochka's older sister. The daughter grew up, and the mother intended to get married. For these purposes, she chose the head of the district hospital. Seledin was married, but this was not an obstacle. She pursued a potential groom with the urgency of a maniac. Only my wife is out the door, Ninochka out the window. The woman is purposeful, she achieved her goal.

From this union Lyubochka was born. She was holy-li and cherished, she firmly tied Seledin to Nina. Although, there were rumors that it was not without a love potion. Nina and her mother were very fond of potions.

- Do you think you have bewitched? - the friend was amazed. - Just like in a joke.

The daughter complains to her father: - Dad, I will probably remain an old maid, no one wants to marry me!-

— Never mind, daughter, you will take a love potion from your mother and marry whoever you want,- the father consoles.

- Does mom have such a potion? - the daughter asks.

- Well, judging by the fact that I married her, there definitely is!

- You never know?! - I laughed.

- I still remembered a joke about the way to a man's heart, - Mashunya amused. –

A young daughter turns to her mother for advice in "amorous" matters: "Mom, I liked the young man, how to find a way to his heart?"

The mother sternly replied: "Remember, daughter, the way to a man's heart lies between the fourth and fifth ribs ...».

When the laughter released us, I continued:

- They write a lot about love potions. Personally, I have not used them. The most primitive of them contain aphrodisiacs that can provoke an increase in blood pressure, an allergic reaction, an outbreak of aggression. The bewitched, as a rule, is fixed on the object of attraction, which leads to a decrease in efficiency in other areas of life: career, friendship, family. You can get a loser, a jealous person, a domestic tyrant, always dissatisfied with everything. Anyone who is engaged in a love spell is also in danger. He forcibly changes the course of things, spends energy on keeping a loved one. The spellbinder can lose interest in what is happening and his love for the object of the love spell.

- And what herbs are often found in love potions? - A friend got interested.

- Masha, you can even start talking about ordinary food, the water you cook with, sugar. Lovage, thyme, oregano, peppermint, and parsley are often used. Someone uses spices, berries, fruits, alcohol, coffee, tea, and even hair and blood. You can just bake cinnamon apple pie and a night of passionate love is guaranteed. Only store-bought apples are not good.

- Why?

- You don't know where and how they were grown, how they were processed, who touched them and with what thoughts. An apple is a biblical fruit, with which Eve seduced Adam. So, you need to pick an apple from a branch with your hand, otherwise the magic will not work, " I told her a common truth.

- Let's return to Selyodina, ... Lyubochka was not liked at school, peers did not recognize the exclusivity of the pop-eyed "fish" - "herring". She did not enter the medical institute, even the patronage of the pope did not help. It was beneath her dignity to go to medical school like her sister. So she got to the teacher's college.

- So this is how it is! I thought she had only noblemen in her family, no less, " chuckled Masha.

- No, there is a lot of ambition and ambition, in the absence of outstanding qualities and abilities! Now tell me about your brother, - I was curious.

Personally, I saw him once in the spring of 2003 at Masha's house. According to my recollections, this is a rather tall young man. Dark blond, gray eyes, deep-set, large nose with a slight hump, slender, proportional build. Andrey has a pleasant timbre of voice, good diction, which is achieved by special many hours of exercises. He attached great importance to his words, as if listening to himself from the outside. At the same time, Mashin's brother spoke empty platitudes. I remember him as a narcissistic narcissist.

- Let's first briefly about the aunt, then about him, - answered the girlfriend.

- Okay, I'm listening, - I said graciously.

- Aunt Sveta, like my mother, Irina, was born in Kazakhstan in the city of Pavlodar. Svetlana is two years younger than her mother. After a while, the family moved to Novokuibyshevsk. The younger brother Kolya was born there. Mother graduated from technical school and was assigned to the Vologda region, the rest of the family moved to Petropavlovsk-Kamchatsky for a long ruble. My aunt graduated as a catering technologist, worked on pleasure craft for some time, and went abroad. Then she went to work as a technologist in the canteen of the military garrison. She married Vladimir - father of Andrey Pirozhkov.

- How, does your brother's surname Pirozhkov, not Bolkonsky? - I was surprised.

- He took the last name Bolkonsky, before he married Lyubochka, - Masha explained to me, - before it was his creative pseudonym on the radio.

- Even so?

- Andryusik mostly lived with Anna's grandmother and Petit's grandfather. His aunt divorced his father a year after the wedding. In the late eighties, she married a divorced Valentine, who was twenty years her senior and worked as a stadium director. Grandmother and grandfather (then still a grandmother and grandpa, as my grandfather asked to call them) in the eighties moved to the city of Brezhnev, now Naberezhnye Chelny. Andryusik lived mainly with them. Aunt's younger brother, Kolya, lived with them, first with his first wife, then with the second. In the early nineties, Kolya crashed in a car accident. The country was in chaos, and Svetlana and her husband moved to the Vologda region. We bought an apartment and a house with a plot for dollars. Found an apartment exchange for Svetlana Petrovna's parents. So they all ended up in Gryazovets. Aunt did not work, at fifty she retired on the basis of Kamchatka experience. Her husband, by that time a pensioner, got a job as a caretaker at a railway station.

- Well, yes, I understand. What about brother?

- To this day, he remains an integral personality, which is clearly characterized by his first word "kaka". For example, as a child, he stayed with us, my parents and I lived in a wooden house without conveniences, we carried water from the pump, in general, and there were certain difficulties with washing and washing. Five-year-old Andryushenka loved to frolic in the fresh air. Once, after playing, he piled a large pile on the porch and, instead of honestly admitting this to his aunt, decided to move it to a less prominent place. He was so carried away with the destruction of evidence of his unseemly deed that he was covered in shit from head to toe. My mother washed it for half a day afterwards, and my father had to go to get water several times. He's been like this all his life: shit and others clean up after him!

- Colorful personality, - I put in.

Masha continued:

Andryusik graduated from high school, then the Gryazovets technical school, received an electrician diploma. Valentine put him on the railway as a lineman. But after a few years, the boy got tired of the quiet life, and he moved to Vologda. At first, Andrei got a job as a sound engineer at the Drama Theater. Then, in the course of radio presenters, he met a girl, Masha, a student, and went to work at Radio Premier as an operator and presenter. "I caught a star", a decent girl bored him, found a gulena who loves to cheer up with light alcohol, transferred to the radio "Europe +».

Alcohol suppressed shyness and complexes. Beer was replaced by energy drinks. Then heavy artillery was used: vodka and so on. The girl with whom he lived was kicked out, they asked from work even earlier. Aunt and Valentin strained themselves and bought him a room in a communal apartment, where he made new friends, drunks. Although, a narcissistic pig will find dirt everywhere! Drank to a squirrel. Svetlana arrived, treated him for a fee in a psychiatric hospital. I persuaded my husband to get him a job. He raised all the connections, which he did not do for me, arranged for him to host the Vologda State Television and Radio Campaign as a broadcast host. The "grateful" brother did not last half a year, started drinking. At that time he lived in our center in a two-room apartment - an office that was in a state of repair, and there were no drunks around. The reason for the binge was the fact that he "invited the girl to an apartment without European-quality repair, she was not happy with the situation, his genital organ did not get up, and he fell out." That is, we ourselves are to blame for everything! They tried to drip it for a fee. In vain! He got drunk again, asked from work, began seizures, attacked my husband, then he had an epileptic seizure. His mother was summoned, assigned to a psychiatric hospital for treatment. He was treated again. My sister tried to get Andrey to work with her husband in a plumbing firm. He did not want to work, he began to drink, broke an expensive Italian toilet, the debt was repaid by his sister's husband and the parents of this monster. After that, he went homeless and begs, set up a den in the room bought for him, spent the night on the street in the summer. In early 2013, Valentine died, Aunt Sveta was completely desperate. But, at the end of winter, Andryusik - this beaten beast with broken ribs and knocked out teeth - crawled to our house. They let us go to the bath to put ourselves in order, called the aunt. She didn't want to, but she came. I voluntarily went to a psychiatric hospital for treatment, this time for a long time. After treatment, he returned home to his mother, she brought him into a divine form. Inserted teeth at her expense.

When I went to Vologda to look for work, I met Lyubochka. She took him to her apartment. By that time, Andryusik got a job as an air operator on Channel Seven. Unbeknownst to his relatives, except for his mother, of course, he changed his surname and passport, and married Seledina. Lyubochka gave birth to her son Pavlik, extremely painful.

- Still, from such a manufacturer! - I sneered.

- For me it was not a secret, kind people informed me, but I pretended not to know about his affairs. I don't know what he told his wife and her relatives about me, my husband, sister and mother, but it seems that we were presented as terrible monsters, guilty of all mortal sins - continued Masha.

- Aren't you ashamed? - I said with disgust.

- Conscience and shame did not run next to my brother. You can understand my aunt, just to attach this treasure to her, and we, taught by bitter experience, did not strive for communication. After all, then I got sick on a nervous basis, I barely got out. Well do you remember?

- You will forget this! Something about the brother and his wife has become clear. Who else is there?

- Grandfather. Will we consider? - asked a friend doubtfully.

- Naturally! What's wrong with him?

- He took the death of his daughter quite calmly. At first he accepted the second daughter normally, but after the funeral they went to the notary, and she wrote a refusal from the inheritance of her mother (Anya's grandmother). After that, he began to take her home. And on the ninth day, after the death of Svetlana, he said that Irina (my mother) was not his own, her mother walked her up, did not want to know her, she did not consider my sister and me to be relatives!

- This is a twist! - I was amazed. - There was also a friend of my aunt, also Lyuba. What is she?

- Dark horse, you need to collect information, - Masha said, puzzled.

- This is what I'll do, I'll go to Gryazovets and Kubenskoye, "I determined the plan of subsequent actions. - See you in a week!

Chapter 4. Investigation

April 2015, Vologda

Maria and I met again and returned to our investigation.

- Forgive me, Zhanochka, - Masha said in a guilty tone, - but I, too, could not resist and went to my grandfather. On our penultimate meeting, on the day when Aunt Sveta was admitted to the hospital, he complained to me of recurrent ear pains and skin problems.

- Otitis media and allergic dermatitis? - I suggested.

- Not. I didn't understand that with the ears, but on the skin in the area of the shoulder girdle, abrasions that do not heal for a long time. In principle, he does not go to doctors. So, I promised to bring him a Kalanchoe.

- Which one? - I clarified.

- The professional is immediately visible, - the friend said respectfully, - I prepared two shoots for him: pinnate Kalanchoe and Degremona Kalanchoe. Everyone knows that the juice of this plant has antiseptic, anti-inflammatory, wound-healing properties, quickly cleans wounds and ulcers from necrotic tissues, and accelerates their healing.

- No wonder they call him "a surgeon without a knife"- I confirmed.

- I told my grandfather how to properly prepare the leaves for application. A week before collecting the leaves, the plant stops watering, you need to cut the lower leaves, rinse, dry and put in the refrigerator for a week.

- Naturally, otherwise you will not start the necessary biological processes of the plant, you will not achieve a healing effect, - I said authoritatively.

- That's it, - Masha assented. - I did not give him complicated recipes, I only explained how to use Kalanchoe juice. The juice should be dripped into the ear two to three drops three times a day, or a piece of leaf should be chopped, wrapped in gauze or bandage and inserted into the sore ear overnight. It relieves inflammation remarkably. You can also apply a bandage soaked in plant juice or a piece of leaf to abrasions. However, I was distracted. I brought him two pots of flowers. My grandfather opened the door, took the flowers, but he wouldn't even let me out of the door! He said that he had already explained to my mother that we were not his relatives, and he did not want to communicate with us.

- I said so?

- He said so. I used to be a granddaughter, but now I don't!

- Was upset? - I asked sympathetically.

- I will survive! But there must be some explanation for this? - complained a friend.

- Time will tell, - I summed up philosophically.

We sat and thought about our own. Maroussia kept looking at the windowsill, carefully planted by Aunt Galya with flowers.

- How beautiful, - the girlfriend sighed, - and my Kalanchoe after that trip began to wither.

- Did you take shoots from them?

- Of course!

- Gave it with good thoughts?

- Of course, - Masunya was perplexed, - I wanted to be able to.

- And how are you at home is everything good?

- As usual, - Masha looked at me in surprise.

- Do not be surprised, this, of course, has not been scientifically proven, but plants are powerful amulets. Moreover, medicinal plants. How can I explain this in an accessible way? When one person is negatively disposed towards another person, wishes him evil, curses, he lets out "invisible threads", "energy ties". And the plant is able to intercept them, to take a blow on itself. Take care of your flowers; thank them if the blow is not strong survived.

- Does grandfather Petya wish me ill? - asked a friend in a doubtful voice.

- Anything can happen, - I stretched out philosophically, - sometimes in your hearts you say something superfluous or bad wish to a person, and an involuntary curse will come true.

- And now what i can do? - Masha looked puzzled.

- A person, sending negative energy flows, consciously or not, does not matter, thinks about us. But we ourselves are able to feel a lot, sometimes intuitively subconsciously, we also remember this person. Having made their way to us, having sucked, unkind people destroy our mental shell, aura. Hence the anxiety, unconscious fear, illness, in the end, - I shared my observations with my friend.

- How to protect yourself from this?

- One of the easiest ways to protect yourself, using fire. If it seems to you that a particular person has a bad influence on you, think about him, visualize his image, and clearly imagine him. After that, with the flame of a lighted candle or a match, at worst, move along the contours of your aura, along the zones in which you feel discomfort. If after the procedure your condition has improved, it means that you correctly identified the source of the negativity, broke his connection with you. Some people have a strong energy and can quickly restore these energetic, destructive attachments, so it will take repeated repetition of the "rite".

- Worth a try! Thank you, Jeanne, for the advice.

- Eat to your health! Now back to our investigation.

- And what did you find out? - Masha asked impatiently.

- First, for my grandfather. Yes, yes, I spied a little there too, asked the neighbors. The Bolkonskys come to see him as to work. Your brother's wife carries her culinary masterpieces, then cheesecakes, then pies, then pancakes.

- They are courting, then, - commented Marusya. - Let them feed, it seems not a crime?

- It is in their best interest to please him properly. Grandfather, like your brother, is the heir of the first stage for Svetlana Petrovna, and it is not a fact that he will give up his inheritance. We are talking about an apartment and a house with a plot in Gryazovets, a room in a communal apartment in Vologda, and bank accounts, presumably about a million rubles.

- Really? And my aunt was always poor, "Masha said doubtfully.

- "It's hard for an orphan to live." Is that what they say? I snapped.

- The division of property is not an easy matter, - the friend said cleverly, - I wonder how it will end?

- The most curious!

Now about the second person involved. Your aunt's friend, in the world, Lyubov Ivanovna Gaponova, a widow. The personality in Gryazovets is quite famous. Reviews are negative. Works in the Infinity ritual company. He has two private houses in Gryazovets, both are for sale. The first house she bought with her husband when she moved to Gryazovets in 2002. The second house is the inheritance of the parents of her late husband. The second half of this house was sued by her husband's brother ... A muddy story. She lives in an apartment on Sokolovskaya Street; her neighbors do not like her and are even afraid of her. The apartment was received in a strange way by the will of a "friend of one day".

- Like this?

- A certain Elena Ivanovna Roshchina, who has her own son, lived in an apartment donated by her brother. This brother also had two natural children, nephews of Elena Ivanovna. This woman, literally two weeks before her death from liver failure, by the way, as in the case of your aunt, suddenly, was inflamed with sympathy for a stranger and bequeathed her apartment to her. And this woman turned out to be ... our Lyubov Ivanovna! It seems that it is not at all in vain, the neighbors and relatives of Elena Ivanovna fear Gaponova, suspect her of fraud, and believe that someone is behind her in law enforcement agencies. Roshchina's relatives failed to challenge the will ... That's not all! Lyubov has an apartment in Vologda in an elite three-storey building, with an improved layout, also received by will from an unfamiliar woman!

- It is unlikely that we will prove something, - Masha doubted, - but the picture looms suspicious.

- It turns out that Gaponova, working in a ritual company, made acquaintances with women who had lost their loved ones, and rubbed into their confidence.

- In pursuit of their own selfish goals, - continued the girlfriend. - It is no coincidence that she became a friend of her aunt after the death of Valentin Yakovlevich, her husband.

- Snake in the grass!

– Exactly! I remembered anecdote about the same dangerous lady:

– Two friends are talking:

– "Do you know that Lyubochka was taken to

the hospital yesterday with severe poisoning?"

- "Did she bite her tongue?"

– Masha smiled unkindly.

- This lady has two sons, - I shared information further. - Senior Senya lives with her, is disabled, and has mental disabilities.

- All the same, God marks rogue! - Vindictively noticed a friend. - For sins, if not ourselves, then our children or descendants will pay off.

- Agree. The second son Edik takes, according to the testimony of witnesses, an active part in the affairs of his mother, has a reputation as a swindler. And this friend at the time of your aunt's death was next to her, had her phone with her, keys to the apartment. According to Svetlana Petrovna's neighbors, on the day of her death, Lyubov Ivanovna came in the absence of Svetlana's son and took things out of the apartment, supposedly her own, left for storage.

- It is unlikely that these things are her only goal, - Masha stretched out doubtfully. - And what did your aunt have of particular value? Jewelry? Mostly jewelry ... Antiques? She, like her grandfather with the grandfather, moved from place to place all her life and did not take any antiquities and family relics with her. Unless ..., - a friend thought.

- What are you talking about, Masha?

- I remembered about our family icon, my grandmother took her with her all the time, and in recent years she was in Aunt Sveta's apartment.

- Is the icon valuable? - I got curious.

- As far as I know, no one has made an assessment. But my grandmother said that the icon was old, she got it from mother Maria, and that one from her mother Anastasia. This icon has long been in the family and is passed down from the mother to the eldest of daughters.

- Why didn't she give it to your mother, Irina is older than her sister?

- I don't remember exactly, "Marusya frowned," it seems that my grandmother fell ill, and my aunt took the icon to her to pray for her health. At least that's how she explained it.

- And what is this icon?

- The Virgin and Child of the Preslav school, presumably from the 10th century. It is not known how it got to Russia from Bulgaria, but in the 17th century during the Great Schism it was carried away by the righteous to the Volga sketes. My grandmother is from the Volga region, she was born in the village of Bagryazh-Nikolskoye, Almetyevsky district of Tatarstan. Her ancestors lived there for several centuries and adhered to the Orthodox faith, - said a friend.

- Could Gaponova take the icon?

- It is unlikely, - Masha doubted, - a noticeable thing, it will be easy to calculate by it. Andrei and his grandfather would certainly have caught themselves when they discovered the loss. Andryusik is a rather greedy guy. When he transported things from us, he collected literally everything, even the lid from the frying pan, which he burned and threw away by that time. Most likely, she could grab some of the cash and new household items that my brother did not know about. But they don't kill for it, at least people like her.

- I also think it's too small, probably, it will still show itself, - I agreed with my frien.

- The third person involved is Seledina, she is Bolkonskaya Lyubov Alekseevna. Parents are alive; they live in the village of Kubenskoye, Vologda region. At various times, this family received real estate from distant relatives by will. After the inheritance, the property was promptly disposed of. Dirty property formed the basis of the family's well-being. The proceeds were used to buy apartments in Vologda for Lyubochka and her sister Elena. Has a son Pavel from Andrei Bolkonsky.

- A suspicious family, - shook her head Marusya, - besides, at the funeral and commemoration, Lyubochka behaved, to put it mildly, strangely, did not touch food and drinks, provoked a scandal, and now she is courting grandfather.

- You and your sister and mother now, it seems, are not relatives, there is no selfish motive. Remaining: Andrey Vladimirovich Bolkonsky, Pyotr Averyanovich Parokhodov, Lyubov Alekseevna Bolkonskaya and Lyubov Ivanovna Gaponova. The circle of stakeholders is outlined, we will observe further, - I summed up.

- I think they will still show themselves, - Masha pointedly summed up. - I almost forgot! I found something here at home.

A friend took out a jar filled with brown liquid, sealed in a transparent bag.

- What is it?

- Do you remember that in September 2014 I was admitted to the hospital with bleeding?

-There we met - I nodded.

- So, then I started taking the tincture, I got to seven drops.

- I remember.

- Aunt Sveta grabbed this tincture for me; she with her own hands poured a part for me from a bottle that was in her closet. And this potion was prepared by Nina, the mother of Lyuba Bolkonskaya. This substance was marketed as an anticancer drug. Of course, I got rid of the neoplasm, but by surgery, but the bleeding was no joke. My aunt also planned to drink this tincture, but later, after radiation therapy. She was diagnosed with the initial stage of vaginal cancer. The treatment was then postponed to the beginning of 2015, and in February she wanted to drink a tincture from the tumor. You worked in the laboratory, you probably still have connections? Check, what is this drug? - asked a friend.

- I will try, - I promised.

- An autopsy of Svetlana Petrovna was not done, but Andryusik and Nina Vasilyevna, who came to the rescue, his mother-in-law, insisted on this. Mom then talked to her about the funeral. She explained to her that an autopsy was not needed, since Svetlana was very ill, she had cancer metastases in the brain.

- Does vaginal cancer metastasize to the brain? Something new, - I chuckled.

- It's all the same that a dislocation of the heel, causing hearing loss, - quipped Masha.

- Let's check this elixir with the utmost care. Do not hesitate, friend! - I assured her.

It's time to say goodbye. Urgent matters called me home to St. Petersburg. But I did not forget about Maria's request and agreed to carry out an examination of the drug from Nina Vasilievna.

Chapter 5. Non-healing elixir

May 2015, St. Petersburg

The third time I try to call Masha, but she does not pick up the phone. All in business, probably. I read the news on the Internet for now. Anecdote about toxicology. Funny …

Wife to husband:

- Today my mother is finally discharged from the hospital after being poisoned.

Husband (to himself):

- Yes, modern toxicology has stepped far forward ... The recipes that I got from my grandfather are no longer so effective…

A friend answered the call, less than half a year.

- Masha, finally got through to you! The examination of the tincture is ready. You can study the results of the study; I sent them to your mail.

- Jeanne, hello! How glad I am to hear from you! - shouted into the phone a friend. - What are the results? I will never understand all these formulas in my life! Tell me in your own words please.

- Well, in short ... The presented sample is an alcoholic tincture. Herbs are selected in such a way that exceeding the individually permissible dose, under certain conditions can provoke rupture of capillaries and blood vessels, that is, provoke internal bleeding. In people with low blood pressure, hypotensive people like you, capillary ruptures are possible in the lower part of the body, in everyday language. And in hypertensive people, people with high blood pressure, tincture can provoke a hemorrhagic stroke. Your aunt's friend described symptoms such as short-term loss of vision, nausea, vomiting - these are all symptoms of a hemorrhagic stroke caused by rupture of blood vessels in the brain.

- That is, the intruders have been found? - Maria asked.

- Not everything is so simple. The concentration of biologically active substances in the alcoholic tincture is not high, and it is not possible to reveal the drug upon opening. Since, firstly, there are no such opportunities in the laboratory of the Gryazovets district hospital, secondly, more than a month has passed, and thirdly, there are no compelling reasons for exhuming the body, and the relatives will not give their consent. I'm sure all evidence has been destroyed! And on your bubble there are your and your aunt's fingerprints, as I understand it?

- Yes, she herself poured the tincture into a bottle for me, - said a friend in disappointment.

- It turns out, not caught - not a thief!

- How to be now? They will not be punished?

- We, according to your aunt, know that the tincture was made by Selyodina Nina Vasilievna. Whether her daughter Lyuba and her daughter's husband Andrei knew about her "healing" properties, we do not know. But there are laws of the highest justice. Evil won't go unpunished!

- We can only hope for this, ”Masha sighed. - Thank you, Zhanna! At this stage, we have done everything we could.

Chapter 6. The search for grandfather

January 2017, Vologda

Our Christian Christmas has always been a purely family holiday for me. Of the family members, I have only two aunts, mother's sisters. Therefore, I met Christmas in Vologda with Galina and Nadezhda.

In general, the New Year holidays are a strong blow to the figure and liver of a Russian person. We start celebrating on December 25, Catholic Christmas is also sacred for us, and we end on January 14, on the mysterious holiday - Old New Year. True, it is mysterious only for foreigners, not for us Russians. Usually on this day we have free time to watch a replay of New Year's programs on central television channels, to watch an old Soviet film for the hundredth time and again cook something tasty.

I went to visit Masha, give New Year's gifts and congratulate her on the past holidays. Even before she had time to undress, she fell into her tenacious embrace. Marusya grabbed the presents, threw them on the table in the living room and dragged me into the bedroom, which served as an office at the same time, closing the door tightly behind her. Intrigued.

- Honey, where are the salads and tea cake? - I feigned indignation.

- Zhanochka, everything will be, but later, - a friend sat me in a chair.

- And what happened to us?

- Andryusik died, - said Masha, sitting down on a chair opposite me.

- Wait, he was not yet forty.

- So what? - objected Mashunya.

- Let's go in order.

- Today the investigator from Ulyanovsk called my mother, - the friend began the story.

- You confuse nothing? - I interrupted her.

- It was from Ulyanovsk, - confirmed Masha. - He said that he was in charge of the death of Andrei Bolkonsky, her nephew. He could not find other relatives, so he contacted her. Bolkonsky's body was found in a rented apartment in the center of the city of Ulyanovsk by a landlady. The owner of the apartment was worried that the tenant was not answering phone calls on his home phone, and his cell was turned off. The payment deadline was over, so she came with her keys to see what was happening in person. She also called the police. The apartment was very hot; the corpse was lying by the radiator. The exact time of death could not be established, presumably on December 29, 2016. The body is in the early stages of decomposition, delivered to the morgue. The identity was established by documents found in the apartment and photographs from a mobile phone registered in the name of Bolkonsky. The landlady also identified her tenant. The things in the apartment were scattered, everywhere there were cans of beer and energy drinks, bottles of tequila, absinthe, elite whiskey and cognac. There were traces of vomit on the floor, presumably diagnosed with alcohol poisoning. The investigator asked for help in finding close relatives of Andrei Vladimirovich Bolkonsky, so that they would give their consent to burial.

- And where did his wife Lyubochka go? Grandfather? - I asked.

- Mom applied to the police to search for her father, but there is little hope of quick results. Where is Bolkonsky's wife, I don't know.

- Come on, then we'll look for ourselves, we know the address of Lyubochka and her parents. Let's shake our "Iwashi herring without a can," as you called it once! - I suggested.

- Come on, Zhanochka! Only tomorrow, and today we went to celebrate, Old New Year after all, - my friend dragged me to the table.

Large flakes of snow fell from the dark sky, gleaming in the yellow light of electric lamps. Ice covered with snow, and Masha and I safely stomped to the entrance where, according to our information, Lyubochka lived. They dialed the apartment number, beeps are ringing, and no one answers. So several times.

- Did they come in vain? - sighed Marusya.

- I hope no. Look, a man is walking; it seems that he plans to enter this entrance.

I imperceptibly pushed Mashala aside, the young man opened the door with his key, and we, with a businesslike, independent look, went into the entrance after him. The doorbell rang. No one was in a hurry to open the door for us, but it was felt that someone was outside the door and was looking at us intently through the peephole. The child ached and the door swung open.

- Hello, Lyuba, I'm Masha, Andrei's cousin, and this is Zhanna - my friend, "said Marusya, modestly shifting from foot to foot.

- Hello! I recognized you, Masha. Come in, - Selyodina feigned a semblance of a smile, exposing her horse teeth, - just put on slippers.

As without slippers, Lyubochka's apartment was perfectly clean. Not a speck of dust, not a speck, everything is on the shelves. I read somewhere that a manic passion for order is inherent in people suffering from sexual dissatisfaction, or indicative of mental health disorders. It looks like there is a clinical case here.

– This is my son Pavel, - Lyubochka introduced the boy. - Pavel, this is your aunt - Maria Vladimirovna. What should I say?

- She looked sternly at her son.

- Hello, - the child whispered in fright.

- Pavel, goes to your room, play, my aunts and I need to talk.

The boy reluctantly went into the nursery, with curiosity, looking at us.

I wonder how she achieved such obedience from a child who is at most three years old. Now the children went mostly capricious, wayward, demanding. All these are the fruits of the so-called free upbringing. Many are not able to master the pot up to three years old. Why bother?

If mothers cling to them diaper panties, which stay dry for hours, no matter how much pee in them. Children carry these "pots" between their legs all day long. It has become the norm that babies suffer from neuroses; mothers jump around them and stuff them with pills. In the old days, children's neuroses were treated exclusively with herbs. For example, a bunch of nettles on the bottom…

However, I got distracted.

- Let's go to the kitchen, I can offer you tea, - the owner of the apartment kindly offered.

"Thank you, we just grabbed the sweets," I said, taking out a box of Assorted from my bag. God, she even has mugs on the shelf at attention, with handles to one side.

- We came to talk about Andrey's death. We offer our condolences, - Masha began.

- I already know that the investigator called me today. Andrey is no longer my husband. We're divorced.

- But what about the "halves of one whole"? - Can't resist, Maroussia quip.

- Our marriage was a mistake. I thought about it for a long time…

"It turns out that she can think?"

- Now I understand how strange it is that he did not introduce me to his relatives, with the exception of his mother and grandfather. Is it true that he was a drug addict? – Lyubochka asked unexpectedly..

- I was an alcoholic, I was repeatedly treated in a psychiatric hospital, I don't know about drugs, -

answered Mashunya. – Maybe you can tell us what happened after our last meeting in March 2015? My mother has filed a search for her father; we do not know where he is. Find out the whereabouts of Pyotr Averyanovich - the main purpose of my visit, - girlfriend is sharp, but why pull the cat by the tail.

- It seems to me that you do not need to look for Grandpa Petya. He just does not want to see you, - said Lyuba in the tone of a teacher.

- Let us ask him about it ourselves, - objected Masha.

- Your grandfather lives in Ulyanovsk, I called him today, but he asked not to tell anyone his phone number. He said that he did not want to bury his grandson, and that I would do it. But, I believe that your mother should bury her nephew, as I do not want to do this. He caused me a lot of grief! - Lyubochka moaned.

- Believe me, he caused Masha and her family no less grief, - I put in.

- After the funeral of Svetlana Petrovna, the first half of the year, everything was fine, - Selyodina started her hurdy-gurdy, - we often visited your grandfather, I watched his health and nutrition. Lonely old man, quarreled with you…

- Not without your participation! However, I will not interrupt, - I almost lost it, and it's a shame for my friend.

– In September, my husband and I began to

quarrel over the inheritance of Svetlana Petrovna. Andrei, as he fell off the chain, wanted to take everything for himself. But my mom and I reasoned like this …

With cash deposits, they bought an apartment for my grandfather in a new house in the village of Maysky near Vologda, so that it would be easier to look after him. Mom and I pasted light wallpaper there. Cozy apartment, promising area, city bus runs, river nearby. What else does a pensioner need to be happy?

True, Andrei refused to register the apartment for his grandfather, he registered it for himself. Peter Averyanovich was transported, he began to settle down. A house with a plot near Gryazovets was registered for me. The mother-in-law wanted Pavel to spend more time outdoors. The husband put up a room in Vologda, mother's apartment and grandfather's apartment for sale. And then the terrible began!

- What? - We asked in unison.

- Andrey raised his hand to me. He became unbearable, rolled up scandals for any reason, I was bruised. It was so stressful! I filed for divorce. Then I was sick for a long time …

We were divorced only in March 2016. It was only then that I realized what kind of snake I warmed on my chest!

My friend and I involuntarily looked at her flat

chest, almost laughed.

- But in front of his grandfather, - continued Lyubochka, - he was building the same caring grandson as before. I found the children of Nikolai, Svetlana Petrovna's younger brother and your mother on social media. He invited Denis, the son of Nikolai from his first marriage from Birobidzhan, and Nadezhda, the daughter from his second marriage from Naberezhnye Chelny, to Vologda for the New Year holidays. Didn't you know?

- Where, I wonder? - Masha asked reasonably.

- He and his grandfather paid for their plane tickets, there and back. It's so expensive! At that time, Pavlik and I needed adequate nutrition. Andrei entertained them, took them to work in the studio, in museums. It seems that grandfather was very pleased. The husband then began looking for your other relatives, but something did not work out there.…

Although, he deceived his grandfather, he re-registered his apartment in Gryazovets to himself by a general power of attorney. I tried to inform Pyotr Averyanovich about this, but by that time he was negatively disposed towards me. How can you turn an older person against those who disinterestedly wish him well?

- And really, how can you ?! - Marusya grunted.

-In June 2016, Andrei demanded my notarial

consent to sell an apartment in Mayskoye, which my mother and I had so lovingly equipped for Petya's grandfather. I had to agree, but I took his word from him that he would take care of Pyotr Averyanovich. The ex-husband, in turn, renounced claims for a house with a plot in Gryazovets, registered for me. At that meeting at the notary's office, he was accompanied by an unpleasant woman; he introduced her as a lawyer. This Evgenia was all in black, her hair was black, her eyes were drawn with black arrows, she was vulgar, heavily made up, thin. They brought their grandfather with them, he told me to sign everything. We talked with him without witnesses, no one pressed him. Grandfather said that he and Andrey were moving to Ulyanovsk, where the climate is better, the Volga River. His grandson finally met true love, and they want to forget about me and Pavel! – lamented Selyodina. - Vulgar Eugene is his true love!

This was the last spit into my vulnerable soul. Now you should understand why I don't want to bury him? - Lyubochka looked at us as underdeveloped children.

- Love, you have lived with Andrey for three years. In March 2015, you told me about the complete harmony of your relationship. You parted at the end of 2015; he showed you his essence for two months at most. And we suffered from his antics for more than ten years. This is morally. Let's take the material aspect. You still have a house with a plot, an apartment of your grandfather, which will be inherited from his father to his son Pavel. My grandfather is still registered there, the apartment has not been sold, I clarified. And my mother, me and my sister from him, except for unpleasant memories, nothing remained. On the contrary, he did not compensate my husband and I for the material costs of his treatment and living. We didn't even hear words of gratitude from him. However, we'll get by! So bury your child's father yourself. If you are not going to share your grandfather's contacts, I consider further communication to be meaningless, - Masha answered her arguments..

- Don't you have a conscience? - Luba pressed her lips condemningly.

- Ask this question to yourself, - cut off Marusya.

It looks like the visit dragged on, we got up, put on our shoes, politely said goodbye and left this clean dwelling. We went outside, it became easy to breathe. The air is so cold and fresh.

- We didn't even have tea, - I said.

- Jeanne, I'm out of my mind! Forgot the tincture from Nina Vasilievna? - Masha cut a terrible face.

- Yes, I am, by the way. Do you think Lyubochka told us a true story?

- It's not difficult to check. If we put aside the emotional digressions, the facts will be confirmed, - the friend said confidently.

- That's it, Mashunya, stop wrestling with it, - I summed up. - Home! Time to rest!

Today the military council took place at my house, more precisely, in the apartment of Aunt Gali.

- Lyubochka didn't leave Vologda, she didn't wet Andryusik, she didn't give my grandfather's phone number, although she knows,"I listed the facts we established the day before.

"Zhannochka, she didn't give us the number, but she gave it to the investigator from Ulyanovsk," objected Masha.

- Did you hit him?

- Sure! - The friend boasted.

- The man is gone, and here she is breeding the

secrets of the Madrid court!

- Do you have a number? - I asked.

- There is. Only nobody picks up the phone, - said Masha with annoyance.

- Phone number Ulyanovsk? - I asked.

- Yes sir!

- We think further ... who else might be in the know?

- Let's break through to Gaponova Lyubov Ivanovna. I have kept the number, - suggested a friend.

- Call, Mashunya. Put on speakerphone.

- "Hello, Lyubov Ivanovna, hello! It is Masha, the niece of Svetlana Petrovna, who worries you.

- Hello, Mashenka! How are you?

- Things are good! I am calling you for the following reason. Andrei, the son of Svetlana, died in Ulyanovsk.

- So young! The lady lamented.

- The investigator is looking for his relatives. According to our information, grandfather Petya also lives in Ulyanovsk, do you, by any chance, know how to find him?

- Where from, Mashenka? I haven't seen him for over a year.

- Call, please, if you find out something. This is my number.

- I will certainly call if I find out something.

- Thank you bye!

- Until".

Well, my aunt's voice, sweet, fake. I didn't believe her for a minute.
- Get dressed, Masha, let's go.
- Where?
- Let's go to Gryazovets. We will sort it out at the place of registration of the grandfather.
- Let's go, - the friend easily agreed.

Gryazovets, if someone does not know, is one of many small towns with an old historical center built up with pre-revolutionary stone mansions at the end of the 19th century, then low-rise buildings of the Stalinist era appeared there, behind them the Khrushchev and Brezhnev five-story buildings. There is a private sector along the perimeter, behind which in our time gas workers began to build cottages, working on the laid main gas pipeline.

The city is located 47 kilometers south of Vologda. The first mention of the "repair of the Gryazovitsky" is found in the letter of grant of Ivan the Terrible to the Kornilievo-Komel monastery, dated 1538.

According to etymologists, the name of the city comes from the word "mud", meaning "swamp, swamp". But the swampy area did not become an obstacle for the construction of a road from Moscow to the North and to Siberia. The settlement found itself on a busy trade route and began to develop rapidly. In 1780 the village was transformed into a county town. In 1872, a railway from Moscow was laid through it.

The coat of arms of Gryazovets depicts a dyeing vat, since the city has become one of the largest centers of flax growing and the production of linen fabrics in the province. It also engaged in lace-making and the production of butter and cheeses.

According to one of the legends, the name of the city is attributed to the will of Empress Catherine II, who, passing through the village of Gryazivitsy, tried to get out of the carriage and lost her satin slipper in the mud. In her hearts, she issued a decree that from now on this place should be called the city of Gryazovets. But the village had a similar name, according to another version, associated with the healing mud that was found there. How it really happened, I don't know.

There were almost no people on the bus. We chatted a little about nonsense, stared out the window. Now the Gryazovets bus station has appeared! Her grandfather lives very close. We came to a small two-storey one-porch house. Brick house, Stalinist construction, covered with plaster of the once pink color.

- Which windows are it? I asked.

- Those on the first floor, - Marusya waved her hand.

- Are there any other rags on the windows? - I asked.

- Yes, these! Look, the grannies on the bench breathe air. Let's go and ask?

- Come on, Mashunya, go ahead!

The friend drew herself up, gave herself a businesslike look.

- Hello!

- Have a nice one you too! - said the eldest, seemingly one of the grandmothers.

- Can you tell me, is Pyotr Averyanovich at home?

- Who are you? Why are you interested?

- I am Masha - his granddaughter.

- And, his eldest daughter Ira?

- She's the one, - confirmed the friend.

- So, he does not live here, tea, since autumn. He said his grandson bought him a good apartment in Vologda. He probably lives there.

- Is his apartment empty? - Maria asked a clarifying question.

- Why is it empty? Lyubka Gaponova's son lives here, Edik. This accursed person often chatters here at night, knocks on something, as if the furniture is moving. The smells from the apartment are sometimes strange. Not otherwise, moonshine drives? I, girls, do not sleep well at night, insomnia, which I have not tried, but I do not want to drink pills.

- And rightly so, - I intervened in the conversation, - sleeping pills are not a remedy, but only a means for temporary relief of suffering. Taking various sleeping pills simply suppresses brain activity. Sleep pills interfere with the flow of natural sleep, negatively affecting the psyche while awake. Therefore, it is better not to use it. There are some pretty harmless remedies for insomnia. Have you tried to breathe valerian on alcohol before going to bed??

- No, how is it? - the old woman showed interest.

- Please note that valerian must be free of impurities. Inhale through your nose alternately with one or the other nostrils 3-4 times. If you have a headache the next day, it means valerian is working, but the dose was too high. Therefore, in the first days you should take a shallow breath, then you yourself will determine the number of breaths. If you woke up at night, then reinforce the dream by inhaling valerian. In no case should you inhale it before being awake. Experience shows that after the first month of the procedure, the nervous system is noticeably strengthened, and after 2 - 4 months a person is literally reborn and his health improves significantly. This method can be used to treat not only disorders of the nervous system, but also atherosclerosis, cerebrovascular accident, heart and other diseases.

- As you tell it interestingly, you have to try. And also, what recipes for insomnia do you know?

- Yes, I know a lot of folk recipes. For example, you can put a birch broom under your pillow. And for people with an overly upset nervous system who do not sleep for weeks, you can use such a powerful remedy. Make the entire bed out of black material. The sheet, pillowcase, duvet cover, nightgown - everything should be black. And if possible, glue the wallpaper in the bedroom dark. This produces amazing results! People who have suffered from persistent insomnia for months calmly fall asleep.

- Isn't that so simple, everything is black and I'll fall asleep? - The interlocutor doubted.

- Try it, it won't get any worse, - I suggested.

- And when did Edik come last? - Marusya returned to the interrogation.

- Duck, I haven't seen him since December. Lyubka sells an apartment, leads buyers. She brought me on the tenth of January.

- Have you seen your grandfather for a long time? - The friend asked.

- I came in November, went to the pantry to get some things.

- Yes, he did not come himself, his grandson and a realtor from Vologda were brought by car, -

and the second old woman entered the conversation.

- This disgusting realtor, the first granny confirmed, kept snooping around with his little eyes, looking out for something, photographing, even our sheds and bushes in the yard. Pure shpien!

- Yes, - the second old woman interrupted, - they also sold the apartment to Sveta together. With all natural wood furniture. Neither a scarf nor a dress in memory of Svetochka was presented to the neighbors; everything in bags was taken to the trash heap. Eki inhumans! Svetochkin's apartment is also not far from here. Yes you, Mashenka, you know.

Masha nodded, encouraging them to be frank.

- And what are you looking for Peter? What happened? - asked the eldest of the women.

- Andrey, his grandson, died, - answered Masha.

- So still young, like. And where is his fish-eyed wife?

- Says that they divorced in March last year.

- Probably, Lyubka Gaponova is to blame for everything, - suggested the old woman.

- Why do you think so? - Surprised friend.

- She, damn witch! She walks, she lays down for everyone, but it is uncomfortable to sleep. She loves to play off people, to whisper in her ears. How did she put her brains on Elena Ivanovna, that she rewrote the apartment for her !? On her, and not on her own son! Then Elena broke her arm, so she cooked everything for her, gave her some tea. She did not let her neighbors visit her. Ivanovna did not walk on her own, and then died suddenly of liver failure. How to drink to give poisoned! You are looking for your grandfather from her, if you haven't sold your apartment, you can't get away from him! She flew by with Svetochkina's apartment, Andryusha did everything without her. So here he will not miss his! Tell the police about her, let them interrogate her! - Our interlocutor dispersed.

- Thank you very much for the information! - thanked Masha.

- Not at all, girls! the old women said in unison.

- Goodbye! - we said goodbye.

- Goodbye! - grannies nodded.

My friend and I moved away and began to share our impressions.

- That is why this Lyubov Ivanovna seemed to me so fake! Type it, - I suggested.

Masha tried to call.

- You can, Jeanne, congratulate me. I was awarded the blacklist of contacts.

- Drain it to the police? - I asked.

- Definitely! - My friend vindictively supported my proposal.

Maria contacted the investigative officer for the search, Alexei Vladimirovich Zuev, who was in charge of the grandfather's case. She shared with him information about Gaponova. He, in turn, said that he had interrogated Lyubochka, but the phone she gave did not answer. We didn't try to call!

Then we went to visit my aunt Nadya, drank tea, and tasted sauerkraut cabbage soup. Yummy!

Meanwhile, Alexey Vladimirovich sent an electronic request to the local police station. And the district police officer promptly interrogated Lyubov Ivanovna Gaponova. Masha's mother told us about this, who on that day was upholstering the doorsteps of Zuev's office. Gaponova said that "Pyotr Averyanovich has a conflict with his relatives, so he does not inform them of his whereabouts." He's fine, she knows his phone number, but doesn't know where he lives. He looks after his apartment at his request and does not sell it to anyone. The grandfather does not want to attend to the funeral of his grandson, because it is not pleasant to him. He does not answer calls because he does not hear well. Then she called someone and gave her grandfather's phone number, which we and the police knew. Alexey Vladimirovich, in the presence of Irina Petrovna, dialed this number, the phone was answered, an old man's voice said that he did not hear the caller's well. Allegedly, everything is fine with him, he does not want to talk to his daughter, because she is not his own. The detective asked the address where he lives, as it is necessary to close the case on the search for Pyotr Averyanovich. But the man, whose voice Irina Petrovna could not identify, hung up and switched off the phone. This information came to us from Masha's mother.

It looks like the search has reached a dead end.

Aunt Nadya promised to watch Gaponova's apartment on Sokolovskaya Street, since her friend lived in this house. We thanked my aunt for her hospitality and went home.

The next morning I was awakened by a call from Aunt Nadezhda.

- Jeanne, Gaponova is running away!

- In the sense of running away?

- She resigned yesterday from her ritual

campaign; allegedly she was offered a job in Vologda. And today, at her entrance there is a gazelle, and her sons are carrying things. He told his neighbors that they went to Vologda. They will live there now.

- An interesting turns, fussing. I sense all this is not good!

- So I say runs away!

- Thank you, Aunt Nadia, for the information!

- It's my pleasure. Bye, Zhanochka!

- Goodbye!

I told Masha this news, and she, in turn, said that the police and volunteers were looking for my grandfather through social networks.

- Zhanna, they sent out orientations to grandfather all over the country! True, the photo in them is from the passport office, and the grandfather in the photo looks like an Uzbek dwarf - the girlfriend complained. - On my behalf, I also posted requests everywhere and attached a more recent photo to them. You, please, repost too!

- Certainly, Masha! I will copy your requests and send them to all my acquaintances, - I promised my friend.

I have a rather complicated relationship with modern technology, a computer and a laptop are no exception. I'm not even with them on you, we have mutual neutrality. I use them as a typewriter, a source of information and a way to exchange it. Recently, I have also mastered the capabilities of the online bank, which helps me pay utility bills and receive royalties. But among my friends there are quite advanced, to say the least, users. I contacted one of these specialists last night, although, to be more precise, at night.

Programmers, at least the ones I know, are predominantly nocturnal. Remote work gives them that opportunity. They rarely leave their comfortable habitat, limited by the size of their home. Virtual life does not allow them to be far away from their workplace, the mysterious light of the monitor rivets their gaze incessantly. They leave home only in exceptional cases, driven by a feeling of hunger, thirst, the need to get money or to acquire other technical bells and whistles. True, the modern development of Internet commerce, the improvement of teleworking channels and payment systems, allows programmers not to leave their homes at all. It is almost impossible to get to know them by chance on the street. They acquire social ties in their youth with their families, classmates and classmates. Further, their acquaintances, as a rule, are of a virtual nature and rarely develop into something more.

So, my acquaintance of youth, I will not name his name, hacked into the page of Andrei

Bolkonsky on the social network and threw me his correspondence, which I began to study. Masha caught me in this exciting activity.

- What are you reading?

- Correspondence of Bolkonsky, - I explained to her in three words how I got this information.

- There is something interesting?

- It seems nothing special. Happy birthday and holiday greetings, exchange of photos, correspondence with your cousins and brother, children, Uncle Kolya. You and your sister turn out to be bad aunts! Forgotten grandfather, busy only with themselves.

- Who would doubt that! - snorted Marusya. - He himself, of course, is an example to follow.

- Andrey was last online on December 29, 2016. The usual chatter.

- He had more than one page on social networks, - said a friend. - I was once in the Buy-Sell. Vologda "came across the seller Artur Korzhikov, and from the photographs of Svetlana Petrovna's belongings I realized that it was Andryusik who was trading.

- Exactly! Did he have a real surname Pirozhkov? Andrey Pirozhkov - Artur Korzhikov, - I guessed. - Not very original!

- I think that this is not his only pseudonym, - suggested Masha.

— There are some strange dialogues ...

It looks like he was searching for the relatives of his grandfather - Peter Averyanovich Parokhodov. So, ... was born on May 9, 1928 in the village of Yamyshevo, Pavlodar region, Pavlodar region.

"That's right," Maria confirmed.

- The family had nine children. He is the youngest. There is no information on his brothers and sisters. According to Averyan Semenovich, his father, there is, but according to his mother and other children, no…

- Yes, I remember that in 1937 Averyan Semenovich was repressed, and in 1953 he was rehabilitated posthumously. My grandfather went to Kazakhstan in the eighties for a certificate in order to receive a supplement to his pension as the son of an illegally repressed person, - a friend recalled.

- So Andryusik found out that no one except your grandfather applied for such a certificate. Very strange. Do not find?

- Grandfather Petya said that in 1937 distant relatives from the city of Pavlodar took him into the family, because he was the youngest, he was nine years old. They did not want to take the rest of the children. Some were already adults, others were assigned to orphanages, and he does not remember their names.

- So, at nine years old, a person should already be fully aware of himself, like not remembering a single name?

- I never asked myself this question, - Masha thought.

- Here is his correspondence with the grandson of a fellow villager from the village of Yamyshevo. His grandfather's name is Ekimov Grigory Fedorovich, born on January 13, 1928.

- The same age as grandfather, - the girlfriend nodded.

- There is his address in the Skype program for communication.

- Dial, please, - asked Masha.

- So, I'm trying ... No one answer ... And there is no way to contact the grandson of this Grigory Fedorovich, he has not been on the network since December, - I complained.

- It is unlikely that this correspondence will help us find our grandfather, - said a friend in disappointment.

- It seems to me, too, that nothing is worthwhile. Although there are many photographs and love correspondence with a certain Lubkova Evgenia Alexandrovna.

- Isn't this the "vulgar Evgenia", "real love" of Andryusik, which Lyubochka Selyodina told us about? - Masha asked a question.

- She is the most! See photos. She was thin, brightly colored, and had dark straight hair. Eyes are brightly highlighted with black arrows, in clothes he prefers black colors. Maroussia, write to her from your page, she is online, - I suggested.

- Good. I'm starting a correspondence, - the friend agreed.

«Eugene, hello, Maria writes to you, the granddaughter of Peter Averyanovich Parokhodov (this is Andrei Bolkonsky's grandfather). We are concerned about the fate of the grandfather and are looking for him; the information is on my page. I do not pursue selfish goals, as well as my mother, she at one time refused the inheritance of Anya's grandmother, the late wife of my grandfather, did not interfere in Andrey's inheritance affairs. I am only worried about the fate of my grandfather, ready to offer him shelter, if he wants to find a social worker. If you have any information that will help you find our relative, maybe it does not seem essential to you, please share it. I hope you are not indifferent to the fate of the elderly person. In any case, thanks, and good to you. "

- It is unlikely that she will ignore your question, - I encouraged my friend, - and she has such statuses in social networks! The girl writes about karma, aura, and universal justice. Look, answers.

"Hello! I told the investigator about Andrei's death everything I knew, he was looking for his relatives. I do not know the exact address, but I reported the area where my grandfather lived in Ulyanovsk. I saw him once. He came to visit us in September. When I parted with Andrey, they spoke on the phone that day. That's probably all I know. And good to you. "

- Good is good. You might think that I know when she broke up with Andrey? - grumbled Mashunya.

-Can I clarify, they spoke on the phone in December, and you had the impression that the interlocutor was in Ulyanovsk? Excuse me for specifying, the investigator was not frank, as he was engaged in another matter, and not looking for grandfather. -

-Yes, they said on December 28 or 27, I don't remember exactly the day, we parted at the same time, I was very depressed…-

-That is, to say unequivocally that your grandfather was in Ulyanovsk at that time, based on the conversation, and is it impossible? Maybe he is in Vologda, and he is being held somewhere? -

-I don't know, I'm not sure, I didn't hear everything. There is no such habit of eavesdropping. -

- You might think I have this habit - the girlfriend snorted indignantly. - Let's summarize the conversation.

-Thank you for this information, at least we now know that in December my grandfather was alive.-

-Andrei said that the grandfather did not particularly want to communicate with anyone, only with him, so I don't know how and what the grandfather decided. You are welcome".

- Perhaps, nothing useful can be learned from this communication. Grandfather wanted to communicate only with Andrey, she knows everything, she saw him once, - Mashunya muttered.

- In this part, her testimony differs from the testimony of Lyubochka,- I said. - This Evgenia was present at the meeting with the notary, and there was also a grandfather. And it was in June 2016. Thus, the girl claims that on the eve of Bolkonsky's death she parted with him and not in business.

- Sure! If you dig, it's not a fact that death is not criminal, - suggested a friend.

- Only who needs it? The main thing for the investigator is to close the case as soon as possible. Lyubochka is only interested in the inheritance and the date of its opening. Maybe you, Masha, will go to figure it out and avenge the death of the innocent murdered?

- I have nothing more to do! He got what he deserved! He lived for his own pleasure, did not think about anyone, did not deny himself anything. He died in an apartment surrounded by empty bottles of elite booze. Death far from family, an unmarked grave in a strange city is the only possible outcome. Note that they did not find money with him, and in the summer he sold an apartment in Mayskoye for at least a million rubles. Hardly, for six months I let everything down. Although who knows?

- Maybe they found it. For example, the landlady or the police? - I reasoned.

- Or the same Evgenia took them with her before parting, as compensation for moral damage for her "depression", - my friend continued my thought.

- No wonder, Mashunya, they say about money: "Easy came - easy left!"

- Yes, Zhannochka. Didn't deserve money, you can't keep!

Masha's phone vibrated. It seems her mom called. A friend took a pen out of her bag, a piece of paper, like it was some kind of receipt, turned it over with its clean side and began to write something down, puffing with concentration. I went to the kitchen to put the kettle on, and when I returned, Maria had already finished the conversation.

- Who called?

- Mum. Today she again went to the operas authorized to search for the missing. Here's what they dug up. According to the purchased railway tickets, on October 4, 2016, the grandfather arrived in the city of Gryazovets. There is no information that he left the city.

- That is, if he returned back to Ulyanovsk, it was not by train. And in September 2016, he was definitely in Ulyanovsk, here Evgenia did not lie to us, - I began to build logical chains.

- Listen further. On January 11, 2017, on Wednesday, a large amount of money was withdrawn from his account in the 4th branch of Sberbank in the city of Vologda, but the account was not closed, and at least two hundred thousand rubles remained on it. He filmed himself or someone by proxy, they did not establish. An orientation was left in the bank, and employees were warned, in case of repeated contact, the one who withdraws money from the account will be detained. The operatives tried to interrogate Gaponova Lyubov Ivanovna again, they did not find her at the place of registration, and the phone was turned off. The police sent a request to determine the location of the phone, the number of which is registered to the grandfather. This is the Ulyanovsk number to which he allegedly answered.

- Well, now they'll find him quickly! - I was delighted.

- No matter how! The request will be completed within a month. This is not a movie, but life!

- Disappointing information, - I'm disappointed.

We went to drink tea.

In the following days, there was no news on the search for my grandfather. I returned home to St. Petersburg. We kept in touch with Masha exclusively by phone and the Internet. History began to be forgotten…

Chapter 7. Appearance of Peter

March 2017, St. Petersburg

The day did not go well in the morning. Everything falls out of hand. The apartment is a mess; I don't want to clean up. There is slush outside, the sky is gray. Nothing pleases...

She sat down at the desk. What will my article be about today? We need to look through the applications ... So, impotence, frigidity, everything is not right ... Personally, I need to cheer up. What do we have here?

«If you feel tired, sleepy, low blood pressure, then the following drink will help you: Pour 1 - 2 teaspoons of Indian tea into a thermos and pour freshly sang milk (0.5 l). Insist on the night. On the next day, you will receive a truly invigorating drink. Take 0.5 glass several times a day for a month».

It does not suit me. Not only do I have milk intolerance, but I also have no strength right now. Look further.

«Sleep tea is very useful, cleanses the liver, kidneys, and contains many vitamins. Brew tea as usual. After 6 - 8 minutes, drain it into another kettle, and place the steamed sediment (thick) into a thermos pre-scalded with a heel, put 1 - 2 teaspoons of granulated sugar there, but better than honey, 1 tablespoon of crushed rose hips, red rowan and hawthorn and pour a steep boiling lump. Insist. Close the thermos 20 minutes after filling with boiling water. After three hours, you can drink. You will receive a wonderful drink of vitality and health».

You can also try! However, I do not have a red rowan. Well then I'll cook it next time. A couple more recipes and an article on invigorating potions will be ready.

I remembered a joke, just about potions:

- Take this potion, it will save you from suffering, you will achieve peace of mind and you will be happy, - the healer tells the sufferer.

- Why, it's moonshine! - Her patient is indignant.

- Quiet, quiet! This is a magical moonshine!

Moonshine is an invigorating drink! The mood got better. These healers are always ready to offer something. Then I remembered another anecdote:

Market. Granny sells healing herbs and potions:
- Rabbit grass! Rabbit grass!

Aunt approaches: - What kind of grass is so wonderful?

- Buy, dear, feed a man with it - he will be like a rabbit with you ... - the old woman began to explain.

The aunt pays and leaves, smiling at her vulgar thoughts.

Grandma mutters under her breath: - Will poop balls.

What the hell is getting into your head? I wanted to write an article about invigorating infusions ... Someone is trying to connect with me, that is, to get through.

- Masha! Long time no see? Glad to hear from you! - the mood, uplifted by anecdotes, went up sharply.

- Zhannochka, how I miss you! - chirped a friend.

- So what's the deal? Come!

- It won't work now. I'm calling to inform you that my grandfather has been found.

- Tell everything in order.

- I have not stopped searching since January. Wrote to uncle Kolya's children, cousin and brother. They were recognized as grandchildren, in 2016 they communicated with their grandfather, so they could well know where he is now. Denis, Nikolai's son from his first marriage from Birobidzhan, did not answer me, although he read my message. Nadezhda, a daughter from a second marriage from Naberezhnye Chelny, wrote that she did not know where grandfather Petya was. That, in her opinion, I myself should know this, since I live with him in the same city. And after he refused to give her money to buy an apartment, she was not at all interested in him, - Masha recounted

- With these grandchildren it's clear what's next?

- Through social networks, I tracked down Gaponova Lyubov Ivanovna. She changed her phone number. But our people are sympathetic, bad reputation runs ahead of the bad person, so good people leaked her address and new mobile number to me with all their hearts. Only it was all in vain!

- Why? Didn't the police interrogate her with all partiality?

- Interrogated. What's the use? She, as before, stands her ground. I don't know anything, except the phone number, - the friend said with annoyance.

- And what about the apartment in which the grandfather is registered? She showed it to potential buyers?

- She says that Andrei Bolkonsky gave her the keys back in 2016, and she, out of the kindness of her soul, sold this apartment until she learned from his cousin, that is, from me, about his death.

- And why did she run away so abruptly in January, and changed her cell number?

- It seems like she was offered a job in Vologda, and that's why she moved. And I changed my mobile number, because I found a more favorable tariff. Gaponova has an explanation for everything! - Masha concluded.

- On the one hand, everything is dull. But, on the other hand, the hornet's nest was stirred up! Did anyone withdraw money from grandfather's account?

- No, they didn't. And the place of the last geolocation of the Ulyanovsk grandfather's sim card was determined in the city of Ulyanovsk. The phone number has not been answered since January.

- How did you find your grandfather? Alive?

- Alive, all right. The detective on the search called and said that according to the information they have provided by Russian Railways, Pyotr Averyanovich Parokhodov arrives at the Gryazovets station on March 11 by train number 376, in the second carriage seat 39, at 21 hours 12 minutes. My mother was asked to drive up to the place of arrival and make sure that her father is alive and well. True, they told her about this fact on March 11 in the afternoon, she did not have time to come from Kharovsk, so my sister Alena and her husband were there. Fortunately they have a car. Grandfather got off the train, in his hands he was holding one plastic bag, and there were no other things with him. He was dressed in his draped coat, had hardly changed since our last meeting, except perhaps he was still dry. Although he was always small, thin, nimble. Grandfather Petya defiantly did not look in our side with my sister. But, I'm sure, he recognized us immediately, with his eagle vision! A police girl and a representative of the Russian Railways security escorted him to the railway station building. My sister and I followed after them. The girl checked his documents, said that a case was opened to search for him. He began to be indignant that he was not lost and did not ask to look for himself. To the objections of the police representative, who explained that they were acting on the statement of his own daughter, he voiced that "Irka is not his daughter, and her children are not granddaughters." He does not want to know us!

- Here is a beetle! Relatives worried about him, they searched for almost three months, did not sleep at night, and he also screams! - I was indignant.

- The girl drew up a protocol, explained that it was necessary to terminate the wanted case. She entered the address of his actual residence in the document, and while the grandfather did not see, she showed it to us. Of course, I'm a blind chicken, I couldn't see anything. Fortunately, Alenka's eyes are a diamond, and her memory is nothing. We then wrote down this address just in case. Grandfather shouted that he would write a statement so that Irka would no longer be considered his daughter. The police girl said she would attach this statement to the case. "That's good; otherwise they rolled their lips into my apartment. You won't get anything! " - said the grandfather vengefully.

We don't need anything, - I said. - In addition, last year you gave an apartment in Gryazovets to your grandson Andrey. Here I have a photo of an extract from Rosreestr, you can see it.

The police representative looked and confirmed my words.

You're all lying! - The grandfather was indignant, but not so confidently.

- What a surprise he will be when he sells the apartment! - I said vengefully.

-I hope, Zhanna, he realized that he was left

without property, - agreed Masha.

- Did he look adequate?

- Quite. He remembers names, addresses, recognizes everyone, jumps briskly, yells loudly, - her friend answered.

- Well, forget about him! Doesn't want to know you, and don't!

- I'll try, Zhannochka. I would have to convince my mother of this, so that the brain can't stand it, whining for my father, - complained Mashunya.

- So there was a loss ... Now nothing depends on you, what's wrong with him and how none of your business. I wrote a statement that you are not his relatives, and okay, - I consoled.

- Such is the case, - held out a friend.

- Still, I wonder if your aunt Sveta and Andryusik were poisoned then? Or was it an accident, death from natural causes?

- Probably poisoned. Otherwise, my aunt would not come to me in a dream, - Masha summed up.

- Masha, I almost forgot to tell you. Do you remember that your cousin was in correspondence with the grandson of fellow villager Pyotr Averyanovich from the village of Yamyshevo, Pavlodar region. That compatriot of your grandfather's name was Ekimov Grigory Fedorovich, born on January 13, 1928.

- I remember. So what?

- I just got through to him the other day.

She introduced herself by your name to make it easier to explain her interest in Parokhodov and his relatives. And he told me a very mysterious story; - I paused to take a breath.

- Zhanna, don't let it go, tell me.

- As you said, Peter's father - Averyan Semenovich - was repressed in 1937, taken away on an anonymous denunciation. The name of Averyan's children, Grigory Fedorovich did not remember exactly, but the family was definitely large. He remembers Petka well, they are the same age with him, and so they were friends. Peter was a cheerful and kind kid; sometimes he was naughty, but no more than the others. The old man also remembers Vanka, he was three years older than Petka. This brother was distinguished by a puny physique, short in stature, was on his mind, very vindictive. Those who dared to make comments to him, always something unpleasant happened. Somehow his grandmother walked away with a log, for stealing apples, so a week has not passed since her cow died, she ate some grass. He even had a nickname associated with poisonous grass. Which one, Grigory Fedorovich did not remember.

- Maybe a buttercup? - Masha tried to guess.

- It seems not. So, as the Chekists took Averyan, grief happened in their family, the hut burned down. The guys and their mother died, burned to death. The neighbors said they were shouting like, but so no one got out. Maybe some of the older guys remained alive then, they were adults, they could have gone somewhere. And about Petka Grigory Fedorovich all these years did not hear anything. I am very glad that he is alive. His grandson Andrei promised to show him family photos, but he never called back. I said that Andrei died suddenly. He lamented that the young were so weak and sickly today. And we said goodbye to Grigory Fedorovich, - I told the results of my conversation with fellow villager Pyotr Averyanovich.

- Also a long-liver, like a grandfather! Indeed, a strange story, - the friend was puzzled. - They told me everything differently, and I have not heard about the fire. Maybe the old man messed up something? The grandfather is alive; he was brought up in a family of distant relatives from Pavlodar. He also had documents, in the end.

- Perhaps Grigory Fedorovich got it wrong. Who knows? By the way, do you have any photographs of your grandfather in his youth? What if we talk to this old man again, show the pictures; maybe he will remember what other details? - I suggested.

- Zhanna, I have no photographs of my grandfather in those years when he was young and young. During the search for my grandfather, we only had group photographs at our disposal, we cut out his image from there, - friend complained, -

yes, a photograph from the passport office, on which Pyotr Averyanovich cannot be recognized.

- As in a joke, if there is only one picture in a photo album and that one is ugly. Do not hesitate, this is a passport, - I inserted.

- My grandfather said that he did not like to be photographed, although in his youth he was fond of photography. Mom has a lot of her childhood images in family albums, a lot of pictures of Anna's mother, sister and brother. And grandfather Petya is only in group photos, and there, the cap is lowered over his eyes, then someone's head is obscuring, then he bent down, then he accidentally turned away. Mom, after the funeral of Aunt Sveta, before leaving Gryazovets, wanted to take apart my grandfather's photo archive. But he shouted at her, grabbed the albums and began to throw out pictures of Irina herself, her children and grandchildren. Mom then was very worried about this, - Masha recalled and was upset.

- All kinds of oddities in people do not happen ... Never mind, - I tried to console her.

This is how the search for Machine's grandfather ended, I thought.

Looking ahead, I will say that I was mistaken; the history had a continuation …

Chapter 8. Ivan-tea and the road

July 2020, Vologda

My self-isolation has come to an end. Masha and I celebrated this event at her house with a bottle of red semi-dry wine.

We admired each other's beauty.

- Is it normal when such young girls like us are already under forty?! - The girlfriend was indignant.

In a pleasant atmosphere of family comfort, an exchange of news took place, the situation in the country was analyzed, and even the weather received our attention. What? The weather was really pleasing with warmth. Almost mid-summer.

I agitated Masha to get out of the city for Ivan tea. My blanks have already taken up several cans. But there is never a lot of tea!

- And why is your Ivan tea so good? - asked a friend.

- Everyone knows that Ivan tea is the ancient Russian name for fireweed, an herbal plant with abundant narrow foliage and bright pink or lilac flowers. This perennial belongs to the Cyprian family and bears such names as Koporsky tea, miller, plakun, snake, crypt, mother plant. For medicinal purposes, all parts of willow tea can be used, except for fruits. It is better to collect the ground parts of the plant at the beginning of the flowering season, when the flowers have not yet fully opened, - I began my educational lecture.

- I heard that it is quite difficult to get high-quality "tea" suitable for making a drink that has a dark color that is familiar to us, - Marusya diluted my monologue.

- No, it's not difficult at all! - I tried to convince her.

- You collect young shoots, at home you separate the leaves and flowers, you throw out the stems. I dry the flowers separately on paper in cardboard cookie boxes, like ordinary herbs, that is, in a dark, ventilated place. Leaves, if they are rough, I put in a plastic bag and put them in the freezer for a while. Then I take out, twist flagella from pinches of leaves and put them on the bottom of a large pan in one layer, which I close with a lid from a pan of a slightly smaller diameter and press down tightly with a load (for this purpose I have two dumbbells, one and a half kilograms). A day later, when the leaves darken, they ferment, I untwist the flagella and cut them with a knife into pieces that resemble large-leaf tea in size. Cover a baking sheet with parchment paper and spread the mixture evenly over it. I dry in the oven at the lowest temperature, keeping the door open, stir occasionally and check the readiness. When the leaf looks like store-bought black tea, I take it out, pour it into cardboard boxes and finally dry it at room temperature in the shade. For storage, the resulting product is poured into glass jars with screw caps.

- And, really, nothing complicated! - agreed friend. - How do you prepare the infusion?

- I brew like regular tea. There are many useful substances in the flowers and leaves of fireweed: vitamin C, carotene, pectin, copper, iron, manganese and much more. This tea stimulates the processes of hematopoiesis, has a tonic, anti-inflammatory, antibacterial effect on the whole body, enriches with vitamins, is diaphoretic, sedative, slag-removing, bactericidal, improves metabolism, makes bones and tooth enamel stronger, helps to strengthen the spine, prevents heart disease, removes mucus from the body and much more.

- Directly "storehouse of health"! - admired Masha.

– I have heard about this healing drink before. The first mentions are found in the manuscripts of the 12th century. As the famous legend says, Alexander Nevsky went to the Koporsk fortress, where he fought with a regiment of German crusaders. After a hard battle, the monks from the local monastery gave the prince to taste Ivan tea. After drinking it, he fell asleep like a baby. The next morning, the Grand Duke felt vigor and strength. He instructed the local population to collect narrow-leaved fireweed, "in order to raise health and alleviate the suffering of soldiers in battle." The production of Koporye tea in large quantities began during the reign of Catherine II. The courtier of the Empress Savelov, after a trip to China, decided to open a tea production on his estate in Koporye. Tea was made on the basis of narrow-leaved fireweed, and to enrich the taste, other herbs that grew in that area were added to it. A few years later, Koporye began supplying tea to Moscow, and soon to Europe. For many years, Koporye tea has been a worthy competitor to Chinese and then Indian tea. But after the 1917 revolution and the coming to power of the Bolsheviks, tea production came to naught.

Only in the nineties of the XX century, Ivan-tea again became popular, and today it again enters the international market, - Mashunya gushed with her erudition.

- In general, tea is my favorite drink! - I summed up.

- He gives you a reason to eat a pound of candy and a few sandwiches with a clear conscience, - joked a friend.

- Exactly, and better than an alarm clock can only be a large mug of tea, drunk at night! - I flashed my wit.

- They say tea can be brewed seven times. On the eighth, the tea leaves float to look at this greedy man, - said Masha with a smart look, barely holding back her laughter.

- And I was recently told that you must first remove the spoon from the cup, and then drink tea. Like, there will be a failure in love. That is, the spoon was bothering me all this time? - I continued.

Marusya could not stand it and burst into loud laughter.

- Have you taken out the spoon before? Rejoice that you are not left without an eye! - pinned girlfriend. At this point I could not resist and laughed.

The next few days we devoted to the preparation of the most valuable drink, Koporye tea.

Masha came running to me at 9 pm. Literally half an hour ago, a heavy downpour with a thunderstorm ended, which turned the streets and courtyards into swamps. Therefore, Mashuni's sandals and her jeans were not visible from the mud. But she, not paying attention to this, took off her shoes, walked into the room and plopped down on the sofa.

- And what need has brought you here at this late hour? - I asked curiously.

- Mom got a call from Ulyanovsk, my grandfather got to the hospital, they ask relatives to come, - the friend reported.

- But you seem to him now, as if not relatives? - I remarked reasonably.

- Others, apparently, were not found. There is some kind of incomprehensible story ... The woman from whom he rented a room died of poisoning. My grandfather also seems to have been poisoned, but not fatally. Mom categorically refuses to go; my sister has a small child. Jeanne, what to do?

- "Who is to blame and what to do?" - The age-old Russian question. Let's go, let's go! I've never been to Ulyanovsk.

We went to the Russian Railways website, fortunately, it's not far to go, however, we managed to do this not on the first try. The site hangs all the time.

- There are no direct trains. Shall we take tickets from Moscow? - asked Masha.

- Look from Moscow! Tomorrow, friends of

Aunt Gali are going there, we will sit on their tail.

Maria studied the schedule and prices for a long time.

- Will we have time for the branded Moscow - Ulyanovsk by 18 o'clock? - The girlfriend doubted.

- I already called my friends, leaving tomorrow at 5 am. Don't be late! We will have a lot of free time before the train.

- So, departure at 18 hours 9 minutes from the Kazansky railway station, arrival in Ulyanovsk at 7 hours 30 minutes, total 13 hours 21 minutes on the way, - Masha was calculating something.

- Not bad. Take your tickets! - I hurried.

- No compartment.

- Take a reserved seat!

- In the first car there are free, not side, lower seats, the first and third. Take? - Marusya could not make up her mind.

- It's okay, the conductors, the toilet and tea are all close, - and I convinced her.

- Here, of course, more than a thousand more expensive than on the passing one - the friend demonstrated her frugality.

- But it comes conveniently in the morning. We will save on accommodation. Take it. Tomorrow at five I have, do not be late! - I hurried.

- Okay, I ran, otherwise it's too late, - the girlfriend was getting ready to go home.

Masha flew away, and I began to get ready for the road. It's good that I filled a whole refrigerator with food, although in this heat you don't know what to take so as not to spoil. I'll take a cracker, steep eggs, sliced raw smoked sausages, bread, tea bags, sweets, drinking water and a flask of brandy. And then you never know what? Several things, the cosmetic bag seems to be packed. Now sleep!

In the morning we plunged into the car and dozed off all the way to Moscow. Having thanked the acquaintances of Aunt Gali, we went to the Kazan station. To lug around with things in the heat, there was neither strength nor desire. In the waiting room, we studied the map of Ulyanovsk, worked out the route to the hospital, considered options for an overnight stay, if we can't manage it in a day. There were enough passing trains from Ulyanovsk to Moscow, so we did not take tickets back.

Time passed quickly. They announced boarding the Ulyanovsk train. We got into the carriage and exhaled. We had no neighbors on the reserved seat. Not worse than in a coupe! We thoroughly refreshed ourselves, during the day everything was not up to that. We took a little cognac, exclusively for disinfection. They spread the bed. Masha took out some book and began to study with enthusiasm.

- What are you reading? - I got curious.

- Poems.

- How long have you become a fan of poetry? - I was surprised.

- To tell the truth, I haven't read poems in collections from school.

- What happened now?

- I got carried away; I'm studying the third collection. The poems of Stanislav Viktorovich Khromov are imbued with a subtle attitude and intrigue. This is what you are doing and feeling now, Jeanne?

- I am sitting on the train, looking out the window, having eaten, I do not want to sleep - I listed everything that came to mind.

- What would the great poet say about this? - Maria asked and began to quote.

"All the way from the windows is visible
Our endless plain -
Woods, lowlands, water -
There is no end and no edge in sight!
How long can you watch and be silent
And dream of some kind of comfort...
I began to notice for a long time
How gloomy people are from this. "

- Great! Would you like to read it? - I asked.

A friend took out another book.

-These are the translations of poems by the stars of world poetry, made by Stanislav Khromov.

I started flipping through the pages.

- Look, Masha, there is also about the train here! "Farewell on the Platform" translated by Thomas Hardy.

"Well, that's all, the train won't wait,
And it's time for me - to leave forever, maybe...
Enough to grieve and suffer
The distant landscape torments and worries. "

- I tell you, poems for all occasions, - Maroussia yawned.

Absorbed in reading, we did not notice how dark it was. The overhead light in the carriage was turned off, and we went to bed.

Only I couldn't sleep. Various thoughts crept into my head ... Sometimes I have an irresistible desire to break loose and go somewhere ... It doesn't matter where. Probably, there is a memory of the soul, which the experience of previous lives pushes to visit significant places for us, in the previous incarnation. From time to time I notice that in my dreams I speak in poetry. And now verses sound in me.

The train passed by
Thoughts followed.
It's cozy at home, cute
Only doubts gnawed.

The city has grown crowded
The years are starving.
You look in vain for a place
I completely forgot about which…

Chapter 9. Ulyanovsk Passions

July 2020, Ulyanovsk

In the morning we only had time to wash, put ourselves in order and have a snack with the rest of the food supplies. The train arrived in Ulyanovsk. We packed all the things in my suitcase, leaving only the handbags with the essentials. The suitcase was handed over to the storage room of the railway station, and they themselves went to look for the hospital in which the grandfather was.

The city is not familiar, we go, look around.

- Look, Masha, beauty salon.

- So what? - muttered a friend.

- And you read the name.

- "Horrible power". Promising, - Mashunya laughed.

- I remembered a joke about beauty. A conversation between two sworn friends. One: "Do you take care of yourself at all?"

"Sure", - another answers.

"Something is not visible", - the first one says sarcastically.

"This is the point of surveillance", - said the second.

Maria laughed even louder. She laughs like a bell. Laughs beautifully, contagious. I also joined her, laughing and said:

- Masha, I have read the research of one professor of medicine, he considers laughter to be "jogging", since during laughter breathing and movements are similar to running. In addition, during a smile, the facial muscles create impulses that have a beneficial effect on the nervous system. Even if you are only capable of a forced smile, it will still make you feel better. And not only to the person himself, but also to those around him. A smile is a source of pleasant emotions. This secret has long been understood in America and Japan. So no matter what, you have to smile!

- Zhanna, and in my childhood they said that "laughter for no reason is a sign of foolishness!"

- Better to be stupid and healthy than smart and sick - I spoke thoughtfully.

- That's for sure! - agreed friend.

- Mashunya, reminds me that you read there about Ulyanovsk.

- It is a city in the European part of Russia, the administrative center of the Ulyanovsk region. Until 1924 it was called Simbirsk, and until 1780 - Sinbirsk. Founded in 1648. The popular name of the city is "The City of Seven Winds". Unofficial - "Aviation Capital of Russia".

The population is dominated by Russians, followed by Tatars, Chuvash and Mordovians in descending order. In 2015, it received the status of a UNESCO City of Literature. And on July 2, 2020, by the Decree of the President of the Russian Federation, he was awarded the title "City of Labor Valor".

Ulyanovsk is located on a hilly plain, at an altitude of 80 - 160 meters above sea level. Vertical drops in the city center are more common. The length of the city in the meridional direction is 20 kilometers, in the latitudinal direction - 30 kilometers.

- We have to overcome such a distance, "I said doubtfully in my voice.

- The climate is moderately continental. Summer is hot at times.

- I noticed! Already under thirty! - sweat streamed under the blouse.

- Samara time in Ulyanovsk. So, we have already moved the clock one hour ahead, - Masha checked her phone, which served as a clock.

- All this, of course, is very informative, but where are we going? I asked.

- Zhanochka, let's sit on a bench in the shade. I need to contact the investigator who called my mother about the poisoning.

We found a suitable bench in the shade of bushes and high-rise buildings. What bliss, to sit down, stretch your legs, drink mineral water! It is a pity that it has become warm. Maria ended the conversation and took the bottle away. After quenching her thirst, she snorted:

- Phew, what disgusting! In general, so, the investigator said that they are closing the case for lack of corpus delicti. An elderly woman in the country by mistake picked up the wrong herb, confused a poisonous veh with spices. At home I made a salad, ate myself and treated her tenant. Apparently, Pyotr Averyanovich just tried the treat, so he got off with mild food poisoning. And the woman herself, due to age and concomitant diseases, died before the ambulance arrived.

- Wait, poisonous vykh, has other names: cicuta, cat's parsley, vyakha, omega, omezhnik, water rabies, water hemlock, mutnik, dog angelica, gorigolov, pork louse, - I listed.

- Why are there so many names? - surprised friend.

- Because it is one of the most common, dangerous and poisonous plants in the entire European continent. In appearance, cicuta is a harmless plant with pretty white umbrella flowers. But the poison contains flowers, leaves, stems, and especially the roots of the plant. Even one hundred grams of poisonous vein rhizomes can kill an adult cow. But what is remarkable, in small doses, cicutoxin (or cicuto-toxin) has a sedative, sedative effect, is able to lower blood pressure, relieve dizziness, relieve convulsions, migraines, epilepsy, therefore it is widely used in medicine. Also, the plant is used as an effective prophylactic agent against oncological diseases, as it is able to destroy cancer cells.

Cicuta smells good of ripe carrots, and tastes quite like edible radish or rutabaga. The plant is easy to confuse with the usual and familiar to us representatives of the rich umbrella family, of which there are huge varieties, and they all, especially for a layman, look the same, be it caraway, dill, cow parsnip or poisonous vech.

- What are the signs of hemlock poisoning? - Masha asked.

- The central nervous system is primarily affected. After a few minutes, a feeling of bitterness arises in the person's mouth, a headache and severe chills appear, which is accompanied by sharp cramps in the stomach. Then an attack of nausea, vomiting comes, after which there is a violation of coordination, in which the sensitivity of the nerve endings decreases, and then convulsions begin, breathing becomes disordered, blood circulation is disturbed, legs go numb. With convulsions, there is profuse salivation, and death in acute heart failure occurs as a result of respiratory paralysis.

- A sad picture, - the friend sighed.

- An important feature of cicutoxin, - I continued, - is that the poison is not destroyed under the influence of high temperatures and its properties do not disappear during long-term storage. During the digestion and evaporation of hemlock broth, the concentration of toxic substances only increases. But the poison from hemlock is extremely unpredictable and unreliable, since it affects everyone in different ways; it is difficult to guess with the dosage. It is enough for someone to eat 6 - 8 leaves to leave our mortal world, while the extract from the root does not kill someone. There is no antidote.

- I heard that the Greek philosopher Socrates committed suicide by taking hemlock juice, - Masha flashed her erudition.

- This is unlikely, since cicuta is extremely rare in Greece. Poisonous Vech is common in Eastern Europe, northern parts of Western Europe, Asia and North America. In Russia, it grows almost everywhere in low swampy meadows, along the banks of rivers, streams and ponds, in ditches, where there is sufficient water.

Am I getting it right? - I returned to the topic of conversation. - Some woman made hemlock salad and treated your grandfather to it? She herself died, Pyotr Averyanovich was hospitalized with poisoning. And what have you, relatives of the victim, got to do with it? Why were you invited?

- Since the grandfather has a permanent registration in the Vologda region, they considered it necessary to notify his closest relatives so that they would escort him home, - explained a friend. - The investigator agreed with the administration of

The Ulyanovsk Regional Clinical Center, they will arrange a meeting with my grandfather, despite the quarantine.

- Still, it took us so long to get there! - I was indignant.

- We can go to this clinical center, show the documents to the guards, say from whom they will take us to Pyotr Averyanovich, - Masha said, but continued to push the bench. - It's so hot! Come on, Jeanne, call a taxi.

- I'm already typing. So what is written on the plate? I forgot, you don't really see. I saw it. Dictate the address.

The taxi arrived just a minute later. Behind the wheel was a nice young man in a mask, judging by the cut of his eyes, a Tatar. He helpfully opened the door for us. I sat forward and my friend in the back seat. I repeated the order address:

- Hello, to us on Koryukina, 28.

- Have you got sick?

- Yes, a relative.

- I see, you yourself are not Ulyanovsk? - asked the taxi driver.

- We are from Vologda; - I did not go into details.

In connection with this question, a joke came to my mind. A conversation between two on the street in St. Petersburg.

"Where are you from?" - The first interlocutor asks.

"From Petersburg," - his opponent replies. "Everyone here is from St. Petersburg! More specifically " - the first one wonders.

"From Vologda", - specifies the second.

- Where are you planning to stay in our city? At your relatives? - The driver continued small talk.

- We have only one relative here who is now in the hospital. We thought about the Venets Hotel, it is located right in the city center.

- But it's very expensive! An acquaintance of mine rents an apartment not far from the station, spacious, clean, with Wi-Fi. It will be much more convenient for you there! - advised the taxi driver.

- And for the price? - my thrifty "I" got interested.

- Not more than a thousand a day. I'll give you his phone number and the address of the apartment. After lunch I work for myself. Here is my business card; my services will cost you half the price of a dispatcher. My name is Renat, - he introduced himself.

- If so, we will call you, Renat, - I promised.

The taxi driver stared at Masha through the rear-view mirror all the way. She broke down and asked:

-Maybe we should wear masks?

If anything, we have masks, gloves, and shoe covers.

- No, it doesn `t need. It's just that your face seems familiar to me. What is your name?

- Maria. But it is unlikely that we met with you, - said a friend.

- Have you been to Naberezhnye Chelny?

- Long. I was then 14 years old, no more, - Marusya was surprised, - and Naberezhnye Chelny was called the city of Brezhnev. I came there for the summer holidays to my grandparents two years in a row with my sister.

- Did you live in an apartment on the third floor?

- Exactly, - Masha stared at the taxi driver.

- Then I wanted to make friends with you, but your grandmother did not allow. Didn't she like Tatars? - Renat asked.

- She just didn't want us to talk to the locals and hang out in the yard idle. We had a whole day planned: fishing, walking, going to the store, reading books and much more, - explained a friend.

- And I really liked you then. They reminded Alisa Selezneva from "Guest from the Future" - the taxi driver took off his mask and smiled modestly.

- This is also my favorite children's film. I didn't think I looked like the main character. Although my hair then was like Alice's, - Masha thought about it. And I remembered a vulgar joke about first love.

"- I've been in love with you since first grade!

- But why were you silent, you fool?

- I was afraid.

- Stupid! Is it because I'm a physical education teacher? "

Naturally, I didn't tell this vulgarity out loud, so as not to disturb the atmosphere of romantic memories.

We had already arrived by that time, and the conversation was conducted in the hospital parking lot. I decided to remind about business:

- We have to go. We will call you, Renat!

- Sorry to delay. Goodbye!

- Goodbye! - Masha and I said in chorus.

We approached the security post, explained that we need to go to toxicology and the police officers had to notify them about our visit. Then they put on masks, gloves, shoe covers, and we were escorted to Pyotr Averyanovich Parokhodov.

The ward was two-seater, but the grandfather was there alone.

- Why did you get it? - He wound up from the doorway.

- Hello, grandfather Petya! The officers of the Ulyanovsk police told my mother that you were in the hospital, and they called us. But if you feel good and you are all right, I can leave; - the granddaughter began the conversation peacefully.

- Well, sit down, since you came. - He waved his hand at a chair. - Who is that with you? - asked the old man, looking at me suspiciously.

- This is my close friend - Jeanne. She agreed to come with me to Ulyanovsk.

- Let her sit down, - the grandfather allowed.

A wrinkled, short old man gazed at us for several minutes.

He then frowned his forehead, then screwed up his already narrow eyes, then suddenly suddenly said:

- Since you, Manka, have arrived, so be it, I'll tell you everything! No wonder you were named after your great-grandmother-witch. Listen to me and don't interrupt! I never missed my relatives. I don't remember my father. The mother is dead. Sisters and brothers, I hope, too. I myself took the documents and went to my mother's relatives in Pavlodar, I didn't want to live in the village. They warmed the orphan. There I graduated from a vocational school as a turner and did not want to study anymore. In Pavlodar, I met Nyurka - your grandmother. She was so prominent, educated, she graduated from eight classes and a technical school as an accountant, and she came to Pavlodar for practice. I got married, I thought when I got tired of it, I would divorce. It didn't work out. Then her mother, a witch, came to the wedding and brought the icon of the Mother of God with the baby, spellbound. She probably tied me to Nyurka. So all my life I was tormented, I could not leave! First Irka was born, then Svetka, later Kolka. The little wife kept spinning, earning money, dragging me around the country, a Mordovian rogue. So life, like a dream, flew by! But in 2010, Svetka took grandma's icon to her house, and I saw the light as if I felt young, my righteous life seemed disgusting. And troubles fell on Svetka. The son of Andryushka, as if he had broken loose from the chain, took a black drink.

Three years later, her husband died. I did not wish Valentine any harm! I poured him tinctures with wormwood and tansy in cognac, his gall bladder burst. Svetka and I also drank - nothing!

The grandmother, by that time, fell ill, stopped getting tangled under her feet. I fcd her a little cat parsley. She had a bigger pension than mine. So I made her look like a fool. Her thoughts were confused, no one doubted her foolishness, as if she were cutting her pension, five-thousand bills, with scissors. The postman brought her a pension to her house, Svetka thought that her mother was cheating, robbing. And then I told Irka about the scissors, showed the cut pieces of paper. Nobody thought of me, but I saved some money, made some stash. Then Nyurka died.

Sveta began to walk, bother her, rummaged everywhere, found one of the stash, in the bank of scum. Someone asked her! Well, I ordered her to cook a bean soup, only put castor bean seeds into the beans. She cooked soup and brought me a jar, and after she left, I poured it down the toilet. And my daughter got to the hospital in the evening and didn't bother me anymore…

As Irka refused from her mother's inheritance, I also drove her away. There is nothing to encroach on my money!

The stash that Sveta took away, I lured away from Andryushka for a long time. The granddaughter and the little wife had to endure.

Lyubka him, with his mother, both muddy, have long hunted for poison. I mean, since childhood, I have been eating a little poisons, but they could get to you, - the grandfather looked meaningfully at Masha. - As Andrey entered the inheritance, I made a lapel, and he hated the bitch Lyubka, more than he loved. The granddaughter, of course, squandered a lot of money, but did not manage to spend everything. When Zhenya left him, I visited him and fed him a salad with cat's parsley. The alcoholic addict quickly got twisted. I took the money - the granddaughter's share from the sale of the apartment in Mayskoye - and slammed the door. Maybe I would not have poisoned him then, but it hurts me with his searches for relatives, he could get to the bottom of the truth.

And so we together with him and Zhenya made good money! I took goods to Moscow by train, who would suspect the old man?

- What product? - Surprised friend.

- And that is none of your business! - Masha's grandfather pulled back. - I had to part with my grandson; - he continued the story, - only he, the rogue, rewrote my apartment for himself. And I kept Gaponova with this apartment, promised her a share of the sale. She ran, showed people, paid for the apartment. It was she who put me here to live with her cousin. I promised to bequeath the bank deposits to Gapon's relative. Yes, painfully she was not patient, she tortured everything, where are the contributions? From this and played in the box.

She and Lyubka Gaponova only knew about the Vologda account. And I am not a fool, I changed money for dollars and hid it. I only have a few hiding places on the shore of the Kuibyshev reservoir, I like fishing, I know the shore. I have saved up a lot for my old age. Andryushka also completed the documents for my business. But you don't need to know that. Tired, tired of telling, come tomorrow, - the old man began to show us off.

- Grandpa, you talked about the family icon, but where is it now? - asked the girlfriend.

- Lyubka took Andryushkin away. Let him take away troubles! Both of them and Ninka, her mother, are cunning, but they didn't guess why Lyubka was sick !? You cannot take into the house what does not belong to you by right! The old man shook his finger. - After Anna's death, the icon had to be given to Irka, your mother, and after her death, you had to inherit the icon, then your daughter. And Sveta violated the order, from that and all the troubles, - taught grandfather Petya.

- But uncle Kolya, your son, died long ago. Why didn't the icon help him? - asked Masha.

- So the icon is female, it only protects women in the family! If Lyubka does not return the icon to Irka, he will suffer, and then he will die. Yes, she really needs it! - The grandfather looked angrily out the window. - My apartment, which their geek got from Andryushka, she will not be able to sell for a long time, because I am registered there, and I am already more than ninety years old. Who will evict the old man? Well, that's it! Come tomorrow! - stamped his foot Peter Averyanovich.

- Can bring what? - asked a friend, smiling sweetly.

- Nothing is needed, except perhaps a bottle of drinking water; something very hot, - graciously decided the grandfather.

- Then bye! - Masha said goodbye.

- Goodbye! - The old man muttered.

Maria and I left the room. Until they left the territory of the center, everyone was silent. My grandfather dumped a lot of information on us. We decided to take a walk and discuss the news later.

We go down the street. It's hot, already fewer than forty, not otherwise. I want to drink.

- Jean, look what is written on the doors of the cafe!

I looked closely. "Coffee, tea, cocaine. We have 2 out of 3. Come in and find out. "

- Come on in? - asked a friend.

- Maybe we won't risk it? Personally, I want some tea. Suddenly he won't be there?

We laughed. It is not clear whether cafes and canteens are already open, or are they still quarantined? They did not risk it and took the groceries from the store. Then they remembered that they had not yet decided on an overnight stay. I took out Renat's business card.

- I'll call, Masha, your fan.
- Why is it mine? - The girlfriend was indignant.
-Well, he's got a crush on you, - I said.
- So when was that? - Masha snorted.

A new acquaintance, although a well-forgotten old one for Marusya, drove up pretty quickly. We asked to take us to the station for a suitcase, and then to the apartment of his friend, with whom I had already phoned.

- Thank you for everything, Renat! - I paid him for the trip.

At the entrance of the high-rise building where our rented shelter was located, a tall young man of Slavic appearance was waiting for us. Renatic volunteered to carry our suitcase, and the landlord volunteered a package of groceries. We got to the place of lodging light. I made an advance payment for the day and received the keys. The men hinted at the continuation of a pleasant acquaintance, but we politely dismissed them, referring to the heat and fatigue, promising to call.

The apartment really turned out to be clean and well-groomed. The air conditioner worked. The water was both cold and hot.

- Chur, I'm the first to shower! - said Masha.

- Then I'll lie on the bed, and you have a sofa! - I retorted.

The friend agreed. We rinsed off and had a snack. Weifai worked, checked messages and email.

- Masha, while your grandfather was talking, I discreetly photographed him. He did not say anything about his childhood, but he mentioned that Andrei dug something out there, for which he was punished.

- Yes, what a horror! My grandfather is a poisoner, - Mashunya sighed.

- Let's show his photos to fellow countryman Pyotr Averyanovich - Ekimov Grigory Fedorovich, maybe he is alive and will answer our call? - I made a proposal.

- Great idea! - My friend supported my initiative.

I took out my tablet and set it on the table.

- Zhanna, in the last conversation with him you called yourself my name, - said Masha.

- And today I will speak on your behalf, why confuse a person?

Oddly enough, Grigory Fyodorovich answered my call. I recalled who I am. Although he seems to recognize me immediately.

- Hello, Mashenka, I am glad to hear and see you! - The old man smiled.

- I am also very glad, Grigory Fedorovich! I came to visit my grandfather in Ulyanovsk, he ended up in the hospital.

- How is Petya? - The interlocutor was worried.

- Everything is OK now. I plan to visit him again tomorrow, - I reassured him.

- Say hello to him for me!

- I will definitely pass it on! I took some pictures of him in the hospital, I want to send you.

Grigory Fedorovich looked through the photographs.

- He is not recognized here, although we are over ninety years old. I didn't think he could change like that. Hasn't grown at all. But he was a tall boy! And the eyes are very narrow. Maybe age-related? I remember that Petya had a birthmark on the back of his right hand in the form of a star. I told his grandson about this - Andrey, it seems, told, - the old man said thoughtfully.

- But the pictures show that he does not have such a mole, - I said.

- And, really, no, - Grigory Fedorovich was surprised. - If you had not said that this is Peter, I would have thought that this is Vanka - his older brother. I remembered his nickname - Tsikuta, in honor of a poisonous plant. Maybe Petka brought out the stain? I don't know, - the old man doubted, -on the contrary, with age, many new birthmarks have appeared. Old age does not paint. And he looks good, fit, and you can't say that he is 92 years old.

- Don't be shy, you look good too, Grigory Fedorovich! - I flattered the interlocutor.

- Thank you for the compliment, Mashenka! I was glad to hear you and, thanks to the Internet, to see you! - Grandfather smiled.

- Goodbye, Grigory Fedorovich! I said sweetly.

- Good night, Mashenka! The old man waved his hand.

I turned off my tablet.

- Now it is clear what secret Andrei Bolkonsky has learned! He guessed that your grandfather lived under the name of his younger brother, I concluded.

- Is he really Vanka-Tsikuta !? - The friend threw up her hands.

- It is possible that he burned his hut, having previously fed the mother and other children with grass, which made them unable to move and escape. He took the documents of his younger brother Peter, as he was puny and short, and went to his relatives in Pavlodar. Probably, they did not know the children from the Parokhodov family in the face, so they sheltered the youngest of them - my imagination drew terrible pictures.

- Why didn't he go to his relatives with his documents? - asked Masha.

- Probably, the teenager was less likely to be

accepted into the family. Or rumors about Ivan's reputation reached Pavlodar? - I suggested.

- It turns out I didn't know my grandfather at all? - complained the girlfriend.

- But sins followed him in childhood, and then he did not show his criminal nature until 2013, if you believe his story.

- And in 2013, he poisoned Valentin Yakovlevich, the husband of Aunt Sveta, accidentally exceeding the dosage of the infusion of wormwood with tansy, - Masha put in her word.

- He pissed your grandmother solely so that she would not interfere with his life for his own pleasure and save money for old age, - I continued our reflections. - He deliberately poisoned Svetlana Petrovna - his daughter, who took part of his savings from him and, perhaps, did not abandon her mother's inheritance.

- I mixed castor bean seeds into the beans, "her friend muttered thoughtfully. - And what do they look like beans?

- Indeed, they are similar. Castor oil plant is an oil, medicinal and ornamental plant of the Euphorbia family. In countries with a temperate climate, this is an annual plant up to 2 - 5 meters high with erect, branched, hollow inside, pink, red, purple or almost black stems, covered with a gray waxy bloom. Castor bean leaves are large, 30 - 80 centimeters long, deeply cut, pointed, unevenly toothed, dull green with petioles 20 - 60 centimeters long. In summer, racemose inflorescences of green flowers with a red tint appear. The fruit is a spherical glabrous or spiny capsule up to 3 centimeters in diameter. Mature seeds are oval in shape. The seed coat is smooth, shiny, variegated, mosaic. Depending on the type of castor bean, the mosaic can be brown or pink. The seed resembles a tick in shape and color, hence the name. Castor oil is extracted from the seeds, which has long been used in medicine and cosmetology.

- For example, I use castor oil to strengthen the eyelashes, - Masha interjected into my monologue. - I dip the brush in castor oil and smear it on the eyelashes, preventing the product from getting into the eyes. After 30 minutes, I remove the non-absorbed oil from the eyelashes with a napkin. To get a visible result, you need to carry out such procedures daily for a month.

- Castor oil also helps against hair loss, - I added. - It is necessary to combine freshly squeezed lemon juice, castor oil and alcohol in equal parts in a small container. This composition is rubbed into the scalp before going to bed, and in the morning it is washed off with plenty of warm water.

- Castor oil also helps against dandruff, - the friend perked up. - It is combined with calendula tincture in a one-to-one ratio. The mixture is then rubbed into the scalp. After 30 minutes, they wash their hair. Great result! It turns out that castor oil is useful, and the seeds are poisonous? - Masha was puzzled.

- Very! Usually, castor bean fruits are harvested in the first days of September, and then dried in a well-ventilated room until November. If the fruits are well dried, then with slight pressure, they completely crumble, and two or three seeds fall out of them. Externally, the seeds are very similar to beans. You can only touch them with gloves!

- What happens if you eat several of these beans? - asked the girlfriend.

- The seed coat contains a high content of ricin poison, which causes agglutination - gluing of erythrocytes. As a result, capillary circulation is impaired in all organs. They become clogged with blood clots, hemorrhages and erosion appears. All this leads to bleeding, the work of organs is paralyzed. Of the visible symptoms, the following can be listed: after a while, hemorrhages in the retina of the eyes occur, then nausea, vomiting, severe pain in the abdomen, increased heart rate, convulsions, and so on. With a hemorrhage in the brain, stunnedness appears, and then loss of consciousness, convulsions are possible. Death occurs within a few days, usually after 6 to 8.

- But Svetlana Petrovna died on the third day? - noticed Masha.

- Have you, dear, forgotten about the tincture

from Nina Vasilievna, mother Lyubochka Bolkonskaya?

- Jeanne, it turns out that your aunt had no chance to escape? On the one hand - the Seledins and Bolkonskys, and on the other - your own father? It's horrible! - sobbed a friend.

- You will not envy, - I sighed.

- And then the grandfather also poisoned his grandson, because he dug up his past and had a large amount of money with him, - Masha continued.

- Then Gaponova's cousin for showing impatience and interest in his savings, - I said. - And he used in the last two cases, in his own words, cat parsley, she is cicuta, she is poisonous.

- But he himself ate this veh, - objected Mashunya.

- At the same time, he mentioned that he was accustomed to poisons. That is, he had previously eaten them in small doses, so he became not susceptible to them.

- Just like the famous Pontic king Mithridates, who subjugated the Bosporus, Chersonesos and many kingdoms of Colchis to his power, competed with the great Rome, who systematically took poisons in small doses and thereby developed an addiction to their action in the body, - a friend flashed her erudition.

-Toxicologists still call addiction to poisons

"mitridatism", - I confirmed.

- According to legend, Mithridates became immune to poison. But fate has prepared for him a more severe test. He did not become a victim of insidious poisoning like his father. The ruler was destroyed by the poison of treason. At first he was betrayed by one son, then an ally, then his beloved son Pharnaces, who rebelled against his father's army and proclaimed himself king. Mithridates wanted to commit suicide to avoid shame, but the poison he took did not work on him. Even death refused to obey him! He asked the chief of security to take his life with a blow of the sword. But before dying, he called the measures he took to protect himself from poisoning stupid. Because I realized that the worst poison in life is the betrayal of children, troops and friends! ... The poison of sin, - said Masha.

- The poison of sin? - I asked. I was surprised by the unusual combination of words. There is something in him.

- This is from Scripture: "Beware of sin, man! In sin, poison is hidden. When you touch it, it will kill you: the wages of sin is death." That is, when a person sins - hates, kills, steals, fornicates, swears, indulges in pride and other sins, he mortifies his immortal soul, poisons it.

-Thus, the poison of, for example, plants kills the body, and the poison of sin - the soul,

- I summed up the philosophical reasoning of Mary.

- Exactly! - The friend has nodded.

- Oh yes, Masha, sleep! The morning of the evening is wiser, - I yawned, and my eyes began to stick together.

The persistent ringing of the telephone woke us up.

In general, I am a morning person and I like to get up early, but not today. The previous night on the train and the events of the last day knocked me out of my usual rhythm of life. While Masha was answering the call, I somehow got out of bed and began to put myself in order. A friend burst into the bathroom, where I was trying to brush my teeth, and spoke excitedly:

- The investigator called, he urgently wants to see us.

- Yeah.

- Get ready faster! I have bad feelings! - Masha rushed me.

Nevertheless, I made her drink tea, have a snack and, just in case, pack her things. Who knows how long we'll be here?

We went out into the street. The day promised to be hot. The morning sun has already warmed up the asphalt. Not a cloud in the sky, no hint of rain. In order not to wander around the hot city, we caught a taxi and quickly got to the police station.

The investigator met us on duty and escorted us to his office. On the way, we exchanged greetings and got to know each other. Carefully closing the door, he sat down at the table and began to look at me and his girlfriend, periodically looking at the papers lying in front of him at his workplace.

I remembered one case, how once I was riding in the St. Petersburg metro and a guy was sitting opposite, and then he raised his eyes to me, and then lowered me. After a while, I got tired of it, I even wanted to move to another place, away from the gaze of the stranger. And then, when there were fewer people in the carriage, I saw that he was reading the book How to Recognize a Witch. Maybe the law enforcement agencies suspected me of something similar?

Masha could not stand it and broke the prolonged silence:

- For what reason did you invite me?

- This morning I was informed that Pyotr Averyanovich Parokhodov voluntarily left the hospital of the toxicology department of the regional clinical center, the investigator said pointedly.

- Is it prosecuted? - Maria asked.

- Not. But the case of poisoning, which is in my production has not yet been closed, and the main witness, who is also a victim, has disappeared, " the source complained.

- What do you mean, disappeared? - surprised friend.

- And that means he disappeared! His documents and personal belongings remained in the hospital, and nobody has seen Pyotr Averyanovich himself since yesterday evening. I sent an intern to the apartment of the deceased Svistunova, from which your grandfather had rented a room in recent years. But the apartment is still sealed, the seals are not damaged. And all the sets of keys, apparently, are with us. Svistunova's relatives have not arrived yet.

- Isn't her cousin, Lyubov Ivanovna Gaponova, still in Ulyanovsk? - Masha asked perplexedly.

-No, although she was informed of the death of a relative, - the investigator replied.

- What do you want from us? - The girlfriend was asking.

- Perhaps, Maria Vladimirovna, Pyotr Averyanovich shared his plans with you? - asked a question from a law enforcement representative.

- He invited us to his hospital. Today we were to visit him and bring him drinking water, at his request. I and my friend know nothing about any other plans and intentions of my grandfather, - said Masha.

-You, as a granddaughter, will report the

disappearance of your relative?

The friend thought for a minute and answered decisively:

- Not. I won't. In 2017, he submitted a written statement to the police that he did not consider my mother and me and my sister, respectively, to be his relatives. Therefore, we will not search for him!

- Then I dare not detain you, - the investigator agreed suspiciously easily. - You can find out about the results of the investigation by phone, - he held out a business card.

- Thank you, - Masha took the business card, - goodbye!

- I will accompany you, girls, - the man showed gallantry.

The information about the missing grandfather stunned us. Or is it street noise? The working day is in full swing, everyone is in a hurry about their business, and there are many cars on the road. We found ourselves in the crowd and were confused.

- Come on, Masha, let's sit down in the shade, - my friend's condition began to bother me.

- Jeanne, how is that? Grandfather is a criminal and ran away somewhere. The police are looking for him!

- Calm down, dear, only you and I know about his crimes. And then, these are our guesses based on his words and our logical conclusions. For the police, he is a witness who disappeared before the case was closed, - I tried to console Marusya. - I think the case will be closed without him. And no one will look for him! You couldn't help but notice how the investigator sighed with relief when you refused to file a relative wanted list?

- And how is a grandfather without things, without documents? - Worried girlfriend.

- Do you remember, he said that Andrey, your cousin, got him some documents, - I reminded.

- Exactly, they were doing illegal things together, my grandfather was transporting something, - Masha began to remember.

- I'm afraid that drugs,- I expressed my suspicions.

- It is better for us not to know about their affairs, - her friend closed her eyes.

- We know less, sleep better, - I agreed.

- And the grandfather has money, he boasted of his hiding places, - Maria recalled.

- Yes, and he probably prepared an alternate airfield for himself, - I suggested.

- Let him live as he knows! This is no longer our business, - said the friend angrily.

- Well, yes, he does not threaten you and your relatives, because you do not need anything from him. He hid from Gaponova, and it is unlikely that she would suspect him of poisoning her sister, - I reasoned.

- Even if he suspects, he will not prove anything, - Marusya grunted.

- Only Lyubochka Bolkonskaya has reason to look for him, because until she releases him from the apartment in Gryazovets, she will not be able to sell the property.

- So let her head ache about it! - Masha snorted.

- And it's time for us to return to Vologda, - I decided.

I contacted the owner of the apartment. We took things and returned the keys to him.

There were no problems with tickets for passing trains. We reached Vologda safely.

Thus ended our investigation, which stretched over several years.

EPILOGUE

I do not know anything about the further fate of Pyotr Averyanovich Parokhodov. He disappeared without a trace from the hospital in the city of Ulyanovsk in July 2020.

Masha is doing well; all her relatives are in perfect order. They are pursued by good luck in all endeavors!

But I often catch myself thinking that like her grandfather, seemingly harmless, cute old people, can live somewhere near us. They walk with us along the same streets, shop in stores, plant flowers in the yard.

Masha said that her grandfather was a noble gardener. In our north, he grew grapes, melons, watermelons. And he especially liked various beautiful, exotic plants, castor oil plants, for example.

However, I will not talk about him anymore. He's not the only villain in our history to escape the punishment he deserves. There are also Seledins and Gaponova ... But the earthly judgment is not a measure of universal justice. They, one way or another, will get what they deserve!

Paracelsus is credited with the statement: "Everything is poison, everything is medicine; both are determined by the dose. " According to this saying, you can treat with anything, even with poisons, if the dose is correctly determined.

But not many people know that the original says otherwise: "All things are poison, and there is nothing without poison, only a dose makes a thing non-poisonous." It turns out that Paracelsus meant that, if you wish, you can poison with anything, if you choose the right dose.

The most insidious poison, as I understood from this story, is sin, because it is he who imperceptibly poisons our soul. Unfortunately, there is no antidote to this poison. Everyone ultimately gets what they deserve!

From the villain's potion
Death is easy
But we poison ourselves
The poison of sin.

A detective story, irony, interesting facts about plants and mushrooms, mysticism - you will find all this in the book by Svetlana Konantseva.

S. Konantseva

The poison of sin
Ironic phytodetective

Illustrations by H. Bidstrup, A. Vinogradov

Editor A. Vinogradov

All events and characters are fictional, coincidences are accidental.